OCOEE!

Published by Bardolf & Company

OCOEE!

ISBN 978-1-938842-34-4

Copyright © 2017, 2023 Myra Kinnie and Gail Waxman

For information write:

Bardolf & Company
www.bardolfandcompany.com
941-232-0113

To get in touch with the authors, write or e-mail:

SISTERS 2, LLC
105 West Plant Street, Suite 3
Winter Garden, FL 34787
myragail2@gmail.com
www.OcoeeNovel.com

Printed in the United States of America

Cover design by Shawcreative
www.shawcreative.com

To
Cora's Daughter

OCOEE!

Myra Kinnie & Gail Waxman

Bardolf & Company
Sarasota, Florida

CONTENTS

To the living we owe respect,
but to the dead we owe only the truth.

—Voltaire

PROLOGUE

What I remember most about my great grandmother, Georgia Brightwell Kambel Stevens, was her compassion and indomitable spirit. She treated everyone with kindness and courtesy, but if you crossed her, watch out! She would become fierce as a cat protecting her young, and she had a tongue on her that made grown men quake in their shoes.

G'ma, as everyone called her, was small of stature and had a girlish figure, lean and pretty, to the end. She also had beautiful, searching, deep blue eyes. When my parents got married, she took a real shine to my mom despite her being a Yankee from upstate New York. Perhaps G'ma recognized a kindred spirit, someone who had relocated for love and chosen to live among strangers, the way she had done herself when she followed Great Grandpa Vernon out of Florida to Virginia.

G'ma didn't show much interest in me until I was about ten years old. One afternoon when we were visiting her at her home in Lynchburg, she asked what I wanted to be when I grew up, and when I said, "A writer," she fixed her blue eyes on me as if she was seeing me for the first time. It felt like she was gazing deep into my heart.

From then on things changed. She made a point to engage me in conversations. She liked to tease me, asking how many new boyfriends I had. Later, when I went to Duke University and decided to study American History, over the objections of my dad, she came to my support. Once she was in my corner, the subject was settled.

G'ma managed to live by herself, with some outside help, and remained sharp-witted to the end. In fact, I had talked with her on the phone a week earlier about my graduate studies and the difficulty I had trying to figure out what to write my master's thesis about. But one morning in late April of 2004, she had a stroke and died two days later without regaining consciousness. Although she was 98, it took all of us by surprise. None of us expected it because she was always so full of life.

I burst into tears when my Dad called me in Durham to tell me the news.

But the real shocker was that, according to Uncle O.G., Dad's brother, G'ma had specified in her will that she wanted to be buried in the family plot in Ocoee, Florida next to her Papa, Grandpa and sister Lizzie. At first, no one could figure out why, but the reason was real simple. Before she met her husband, Vernon, he had been in the Navy and always wanted to be buried at sea. When he died, G'ma fulfilled his wish, but she wasn't going to have that done for her, no matter how much she loved him. She had no real connection to his folks in Virginia, so she decided to return to Ocoee after being gone for nearly eighty years. Besides, no one was going to disobey her wishes, not even after she was no longer with us!

So we all flew down to Florida from Charlotte—Mom, Dad, my younger brother, Connor, and me. Upon arrival, we rented separate cars at the airport because I was going to leave before them. I had to get back for finals. Then we drove to Ocoee, a small town about 15 miles to the west of Orlando. It was a quiet, suburban looking place with a big lake in the middle.

We met a slew of relatives I'd never seen or heard of before. Most of them belonged to the Pike clan, a wealthy, old, established Ocoee family that owned a great deal of property in the area, notably orange groves and vegetable fields. Apparently G'ma's older sister, Janie, had married one of the Pikes who had become the head of the family during a time of expansion and had guided it to prosperity. I got to say hello to a whole bunch of cousins, many of them older than me. They were all friendly and polite, in a distant kind of way, and couldn't understand why a relative none of them really knew wanted to be laid to rest in their town. We sort of knew, but it turned out there was more to it than any of us were aware of at the time.

That night at the hotel, Mom pulled out a large book from her suitcase and told me that G'ma Georgia had asked her to give this to me when she was no longer with us. It looked like an old ledger, and I gave it no more than a glance because we were about to go to dinner with some of our relatives.

The funeral service was held the next morning at the Ocoee Christian Church, which was on the National Register. It was a charming, white edifice with a tall, narrow, pointed steeple. We were told that it had been originally dedicated in 1891 and was the oldest Christian church in continuous use in Florida. To our surprise, it was filled with people.

The interior was lovely, with worn, wooden pews and rafters, and three beautiful stained glass windows behind the altar. The sunlight shining through gave them a golden glow which, I imagined, enveloped G'ma on her way to heaven. Not that she had been a saint, but I believed she deserved that kind of send-off.

The pastor, not having had G'ma as a member of the congregation, gave a sermon, touching on the highlights of her life. He'd been given a list by my uncle ahead of time, but didn't capture any of her unique, spirited personality. When he finished the final prayer, however, he asked us all to stand and hold hands to sing G'ma's favorite song, "Let There Be Peace on Earth," and it brought tears to my eyes. What a beautiful way to remember her!

Connor and I drove together in my car in the procession to the cemetery. It gave us a chance to catch up. We weren't that close. He was seven years younger than me and a jock. He'd lettered in football, basketball, and baseball since his sophomore year, while my biggest achievement had been becoming editor of the school newspaper as a senior. He had just taken the SATs and was trying to figure out where to apply to college. He planned to be a lawyer like my dad.

When we arrived at the burial site, we again sat with our family. The minister spoke a few more generic words of comfort and then everyone, one at a time, filed past the grave site and put a rose on G'ma's casket to show love to her.

I was surprised when a frail, old black man, supported by a woman my age, came up and placed his rose among the others. There were no other African Americans in the audience. One of my older cousins whispered that it was a Mr. James Edwards, who came over from Jacksonville and had known G'ma when she was a young girl growing up in Ocoee, which meant he must have been in his late nineties, too.

I watched him as we all sang, "God Be with You Till We Meet Again." He had a surprisingly strong, clear baritone voice but faltered toward the end. I could tell he was crying.

No one paid any attention to him when the funeral was finished, so I went over to him. When I introduced myself as Cassie Brightwell Stevens, G'ma Georgia's great granddaughter, his eyes lit up. He grabbed my hand and said, "I'm very glad to meet you. Your G'ma was a very dear person to me." Then he smiled wistfully and said, "Everyone called me Little Jim in those days."

He introduced me to his great granddaughter, Georgia Mae, who he said was named for his mamma, Essie Mae and G'ma Georgia. I was surprised and realized that there were layers of untold history here that I couldn't even begin to fathom. The young woman was studying at Bethune-Cookman College in Daytona Beach, and we briefly traded stories about being in school. I wish I could have spoken to him more, but when I asked if he would go to the reception, he declined and said they had to get back home to Jacksonville. We exchanged addresses and promised to stay in touch as we all headed for our cars.

My Dad, Vern Jr. and his brother Uncle O.G. had planned a luncheon and visitation after G'ma's funeral that she would have loved. The catered affair took place outside under the shade trees at the Ocoee Gazebo on the lake. Dad spoke to the crowd about how G'ma Georgia always talked about the parties under the oaks at the homestead where everyone could visit and eat, all at the same time. He raised a glass in toast to all the guests and especially to G'ma Georgia. "I know she would think this was a perfect send off."

The family all stayed around to enjoy the sun set one more time together on the lake. At some point, a chubby woman who looked to be in her sixties came over to our table with two middle-aged men in tow and introduced herself as Janie Pike's daughter, Mabel. The two men standing awkwardly next to her were her sons. I recognized G'ma's blue eyes in them.

She said she was so pleased to meet us and what a shame it was that G'ma had become estranged from her family. She'd come down to visit on only three occasions, the last time in 1934 for her Papa's funeral, but she hadn't bothered when her sisters died. I could hear the disdainful judgment in her voice and wondered how G'ma would have responded, but we all remained polite and said we mustn't let that happen again and would stay in touch.

After they stalked off, I said my good-byes to Mom, Dad and Connor, and drove to the Orlando airport to catch my flight back to school.

When I was settled in my airplane seat, I took out the ledger Mom had given me. It was surprisingly heavy. The leather binding felt smooth and hard, and was worn at the edges. When I opened it, there was writing right away without any title page, just a date at the top, May 22, 1925. The handwriting was neat and small with little flourishes, and it took me some time to decipher. It read:

> Last week, Ocoee became its own city, with two brand-new city gates and not a word about the massacre that occurred just a few years back and the bad things that have happened since then, so I am going to write about it, even if no one wants to talk about it. But since I didn't grow up here for all of my life, I'll start at the beginning as I remember it.

I was stunned. What massacre? What bad things? In that pleasant, sleepy little town where I'd just spent two days? I read on and by the time the flight touched down at the Raleigh-Durham Airport I had made it about a third of the way through. It was riveting, and I could hardly wait to get to my off-campus apartment. I stayed up into the early hours of the morning and kept reading until I had finished G'ma's journal.

By then I was bleary-eyed, but also agitated and excited. I knew I had found the subject for my Master's thesis.

After discussions with my advisor, I decided to keep G'ma's account as the core and add historical information—what was happening in the world, nearby and far away, that had an impact on the events in Ocoee. I wanted readers to better understand what it was like nearly a hundred years ago, when our country was very different, and yet also troublingly familiar.

As I worked through the journal, I quickly realized that, while G'ma did start "at the beginning," after that she wrote things down as they came into her mind, skipping back and forth in time, repeating some things, not worrying about the chronology. I've kept it that way when it makes sense, but also moved entries around according to a timeline I created of what happened.

She began with the trip that brought her first to Florida. Although she didn't mention it, I believe it happened in the fall of 1913 when she was just eight years old.

1

TRAVELING

The day we left Jefferson, in the State of Georgia, my sisters and I were up and dressed at the crack of dawn with our pallets rolled and stowed in the back of Papa's shiny Overland Touring Car. Papa had already put curtains on the car windows to keep the rain out as we started our trip to Florida. Mrs. Lester, our closest neighbor and good friend, hurried over with her arms full of leftovers from our farewell supper for us to take on the road. I thought about how much I would miss her delicious food and how much the whole family would miss her as a friend.

Papa said that my older sister could ride shotgun, and my other sister and I, being younger, could have the whole back seat of our touring car to lie down, nap, and stretch out during the long trip. So I jumped in and made myself comfortable next to a picture of our beautiful Mama and the soft, cuddly, white crocheted counterpane from her bed.

We were all still heartbroken. Mama had been dead less than a month. She'd been very sick for about a week with black measles, but we just knew she was going to get better any day. One Sunday morning, however, Papa came into the kitchen and announced Mama had died during the night. We all held each other and cried for a long time.

There were many arrangements to be made before Mama could be buried. Fortunately, our neighbors flew into action. The church ladies' group brought food for every meal. Several ladies sat with Mama's body in the parlor so she wouldn't be alone before she was buried.

Mama's funeral was held Friday morning at the Baptist Church. It was packed with friends from Jefferson, Georgia. The preacher said how much her presence would be missed in the church, in the town, and especially in her family. The townspeople and all of us went to the cemetery about noon to bury our dear Mama. Papa walked around in shock, so Janie said. I didn't know what she meant by that, but I knew I already missed Mama's sweet smiles. During the following weeks Papa sold the new house he had built for Mama and us outside of town, as well as his mechanic business.

The very last thing we did before leaving Georgia was to go to the cemetery and visit Mama's grave. Papa had spent the evenings carving a baby lamb out of wood. He told all of us to gather around the grave and hold hands while he talked about how important being a family and staying together was. He put the carved lamb on the grave, and my sisters and I said our goodbyes to Mama for the last time. After a short while we went to the car and drove off, heading down the road to Florida.

We were going to Grandpa's house in West Orange County, more specifically in a place called Ocoee. He had invited us to come to live with him. He told Papa that he could help out with us girls and Papa could help out at the dairy. That sounded exciting, to live with Grandpa in Florida.

We all yelled "Yippee" when we crossed the Georgia-Florida line. By then we had been up for a very long time and I was getting tired, so I covered up with Mama's counterpane, which still smelled like her lavender soap. Thoughts of my family and stories swirled in my head.

Our Papa, Edward Asbury Kambel, and our Mama, Cora Mable Griffin Kambel, were married in Georgia and had lived around Jefferson for many years. He was a very good looking man who stood six-feet-two in his stocking feet and weighed two-hundred-forty pounds. He had sky blue eyes and a fair complexion. His hair had turned prematurely white when he was sixteen years old. That may seem unusual, but it ran in the family. He told us that the same thing had happened to his sister.

A quiet man, Papa generally spoke only when he had something to say. He was a hard worker and an avid sportsman, with hunting and fishing at the top of his list of his favorite activities. He was straight laced, especially around us girls. Since Mama died there was sadness in his eyes because she had been the love of his life. He loved us girls, too, and would do anything to protect us and keep us together.

My sister Cora Jane—everyone called her Janie—was fifteen and mostly interested in boys. Elizabeth Grace—Lizzie—was nine, quiet-like and serious-minded. Although she was a year older than me, she wasn't as curious or adventurous. She liked to boss me around, though, claiming she had to look after me because I couldn't take care of myself.

Grandpa William David Kambel had lived in Ocoee for many years. Our Grandma, Mary Jane, had died several years earlier and Grandpa stayed on to keep working his dairy, which was near the homestead at Starke Lake. Papa had visited him from time to time, but we had never been, and now it would be our new home.

Papa told us that Grandpa met Dr. James Starke in 1864 when they were both soldiers fighting in the Civil War. Ten years earlier, a decade after Florida had been admitted as a slave state to the United States, Dr. Starke, who was originally from South Carolina, had bought land in Central Florida at

South Apopka. He, along with his hundred or so slaves, had grown cotton for a money crop and vegetables for the table. There was always plenty of food, what with wild animals to hunt and all kinds of fish to catch in the many area lakes.

After a while there was a big problem when Dr. Starke's field workers began to get sick and die from malaria. So, he went seven miles to the east and found a beautiful spring-fed lake, which he named after himself. His workers could go there at nighttime to sleep free from mosquitoes. They would return to tending the crops the next day at South Apopka. This proved to be a wonderful solution.

Close to the end of the War Between the States, the Confederates called on Dr. Starke to bring a brigade of soldiers to fight. He immediately enlisted a bunch of local men, moved his slaves to the west side of Lake Apopka, and left his land behind. The custom at the time was to free the slaves when a landowner left. According to Grandpa, that's what Dr. Starke did.

Grandpa and Dr. Starke were at the same camp during the Civil War and became friends, although Dr. Starke was at least ten years older. Then Jake Summerlin arrived at the camp from Florida with cattle for the Confederates. Grandpa liked Jake and rode with him on other cow drives while he was still a soldier. He even made a trip to Cuba with him. Jake liked doing business there because he felt the Spanish had real money, not just paper notes like the Confederacy, with all the war debt and money being scarce.

After General Lee and General Grant agreed to stop fighting and the Civil War ended, Grandpa went back to Florida and bought land at South Apopka from his friend, Dr. Starke. He also made money with Jake Summerlin in the cow business. With the land he bought from Dr. Starke, he started his dairy "scot-free," as he liked to say, referring to his Scotch-Irish heritage.

Grandpa spoke a lot about the Kambel Coat of Arms and showed it off on the front sign of the Dairy. He once told me that it was used to identify members of the family on the battle-field and at home. His chest would puff out with pride whenev-er he talked about his old country ancestors.

I woke up when Janie in the front seat asked where we could stop and eat lunch. Papa told her just a few miles down the road there was a clump of beautiful pecan trees in Alachua, where we would have shade. Sure enough, we soon got there, and he pulled over, telling us to get out the food that Mrs. Les-ter had given us. He took a walk. We all thought he had to go to the bathroom. We did too, but we could wait.

When he returned, we all ate our delicious chicken and dumplings and drank sweet tea. Papa said that he was going to take a nap to rest up to finish the drive. Janie, Lizzie and I went out to the woods to go to the bathroom. Then we walked around the area sipping our tea and talking and laughing. At some point, we heard sounds coming from a clearing to the left of us. We walked over very quietly and saw a circle of black children dancing with one child in the center clapping her hands and singing:

> *Fry the meat, you give me the skin,*
> *and that's where my mama's trouble begin.*
> *Then you Juba up, Juba down,*
> *Juba all around town.*

The black kids saw us and stopped. We wanted to know how to do the Juba dance. They wanted a drink of our tea, so we shared our cups with them.

But then a white man came into the clearing from the cotton field. He was mad as a fighting bull and shouted for the "pick-a-ninnies" to get back to pickin' cotton. Then he yelled at us, "Do you think they are as good as you?" He pointed his finger at my sisters and me, and yelled some more: "You have no business playing with nigger children. Take your cups and leave. Didn't your daddy and mama teach you nuthin'?"

We ran like the wind back to the car. I was scared, but I still wanted to know about that dance. Papa was up, looking rested. After we got in he started the car, and off we went. Lizzie and I looked at each other but didn't breathe a word about what just had happened. We took the Sears Catalogue and tore out ladies and children and played paper dolls for a while. Then we told stories.

By now it was pitch dark and with the car lights on we could see the shapes of orange trees around us. We knew we were getting close to Grandpa's place.

When we arrived, Grandpa helped us into the house and showed us to our rooms. We were so tired all of us girls went straight to bed.

After a good night's sleep, we saw that Grandpa had screened one side of the front porch to make a sleeping porch for us. Lizzie and I had bunk beds on one side of the room and Janie had a private area on the other all to herself.

We had breakfast in the kitchen and then went to the big sitting room on the lakeside where Grandpa welcomed us formally, like a true southern gentleman. I thought, "We are so blessed to have our Grandpa." Although a little shorter than Papa, with his military bearing, he could seem intimidating, and when he entered a room his presence was profound. Like Papa, his eyes were sky blue and he had a fair complexion, but his hair and long beard were white as cotton. He was kind, loving, and gentle when it came to us girls. When he reminisced about our Mama, he'd say," She was a beautiful, lovable lady and the perfect daughter-in-law."

We arrived on Friday, so Saturday Grandpa had a hoedown for us to meet people around the area. He and some of the local men had been to Hackney Prairie Lake and caught many huge breams. They'd also cut swamp cabbage so we could enjoy this lip smack'en dish.

The men prepared the fish and fried them in big wash pots on an open fire. The ladies cooked the cabbage and made up hush puppy batter to fry. Several young men set up tables outside under the big oak trees for the food, and many of the kids played in the area. Some of the more adventuresome youngsters ran down by the lake and waded in the shallow edge.

When everything was ready, Grandpa rang the big dinner bell and everyone came to the tree shaded area for dinner. He took this opportunity to introduce us all to each other, one by one. It made me feel self-conscious, but the guests all welcomed us with such warmth I felt like this truly was our new home.

After supper, I asked one of the men why the fried bread was called hush puppies. He laughed and said, "I thought everyone knew that. When men go camping and cook over a campfire and the dogs are howling and barking for food, they throw fried corn meal to them and yell, 'Hush puppies!'"

It was a good story that made perfect sense to me, but I didn't know whether it was true or not.

One of the visiting boys, Ned Douglas, who had buck teeth, freckles, and bright red hair, told us he was fixin' to sneak around the outside to the kitchen window and pick the pecans off the cakes that had been set out to cool. He pointed to Lizzie and me and said, "If you two new kids don't help me, you can't have any pecans and I'll say I saw you do it!" So we quickly decided to go along and help, all the while praying we would not get caught. When the cakes were served, everyone wondered what happened to the nuts. We played all innocent and were happy when someone said, "The squirrels probably took 'em."

With all the people visiting and talking with one another, I noticed a little black boy who was alone in the kitchen. I felt sorry that he did not have anyone to play with and went over to him. When I asked him his name, he said, "Little Jim, after my dad, Big Jim." Then he pointed to a slender woman with her black hair pulled away from her face, busy serving dessert outside. "And that's my mama."

At some point, she came into the kitchen, wiping her hands on her apron. When she saw us talking, she nodded to me and gave me a brief smile. That was my first encounter with Essie Edwards, our cook, who became an important person in our lives. Her husband, Big Jim, was at least six feet tall, not fat but muscular from heavy work. He always had a smile, soft voice and a very pleasant manner. Essie could be persnickety.

She was always kind to us, though, and Boy, oh, Boy she was a great cook.

G'ma's journey to Florida, however, was not unusual, even though it came about because her mother had died. She, her father and her sisters were part of a great migration that had started after the Civil War and continued into the early 1900s. At first it was soldiers from the defeated rebel army, soon joined by others who wanted to escape the carpetbagger Yankees during Reconstruction.

In those days Florida was still something of a place for pioneers. Unlike the other Southern States, Florida hadn't been directly involved in the Civil War, so it wasn't subject to the same economic and political difficulties that came with Reconstruction.

An early arrival was Lieutenant Bluford Marion Sims from Tennessee, later known as "Captain Sims" and considered the founder of Ocoee. He apparently named the area after a river near where he grew up, which meant "no cold" in Cherokee.

People were drawn to what was then known as Mosquito County, later changed to Orange County, and farmed the fertile soil in unincorporated areas around Orlando by Lake Apopka—Oakland, Winter Garden and Ocoee—each with their unique characteristics. Oakland was a posh place where the wealthy people in the area lived in mansions, many of them on the lake. Winter Garden was more of a working town with a small black population. Ocoee was, for the most part, a farming community, in which African American and white inhabitants were nearly equal in numbers, and a number of blacks owned their homes.

Well-to-do white settlers came in fancy horse-drawn carriages. Their household goods would follow on wagon trains heaped high with their belongings and pulled by oxen or mules. Others brought little more than the clothes on their backs. But they all had high hopes to make a better life for themselves and their families. They found like-minded, hard-working folks, rich agricultural soil, and a sizable free black population used to toil in the fields.

Later with the backlash against Reconstruction and the beginnings of Jim Crow, more blacks moved south, looking for better opportunities than they had in the impoverished states to the north.

The arrival of the railroad in 1890, directly connecting Ocoee to the east coast of Florida and the northern states, improved the economy further, despite a crippling freeze the year before. While it took time for the orange industry to recover, crops like celery, and other vegetables continued to find eager buyers from up north, turning Ocoee into a prosperous town.

2

SETTLING IN

After our long trip and another late night, we wanted to sleep in, but Grandpa wouldn't hear of it. "Sunday is for church," he said. So Papa woke us up early and we got ready, even with our bleary eyes. Grandpa took us to Winter Garden in the touring car to the large wooden Baptist church. He went there because Grandma had been a Baptist and loved it. He said, "Every time I go into that church I can feel your Grandma's presence."

The preacher talked about Mother's Day, which was started by Anna Jarvis, a Methodist. I felt that it celebrated Mama even though she was not there with us but in heaven. It was a pretty church and I could see why our grandma had loved it. Janie met some young people her age who invited her to visit them after church in Oakland.

On our way home Grandpa took a roundabout way to show us the Ocoee Christian Church and tell us the story of how it was built. Colonel Withers, one of the early settlers of Ocoee, had gotten Captain Sims to donate the land at the corner of Bluford and Magnolia Avenues. He then set out to make plans and decided on the building materials. Nothing but the best would do. The beautiful stained glass windows were shipped from Belgium to Jacksonville down the St. Johns

River to Sanford and from there by ox cart to Ocoee without a single scratch. The bell was one of five clarion bells taken from a tower in London, England. Colonel Withers wanted the ceilings to have high pointed arches in the Gothic style and the floor plan to be in the shape of a cross. The entire wooden interior was made from the center portions of heartland pine trees with rounded knots like acorns at the end. Hanging kerosene lamps provided soft lighting for day and night services, as well as weddings and revivals.

Colonel Withers never got to enjoy all the beauty that he had painstakingly created because he died before it was completed. Grandpa ended his story by saying that the church had been dedicated on May 19, 1891 "to the glory of God and in Colonel Withers memory."

Grandpa drove us around some more, and when we got home, I got a good look at our house. It was a one-story cracker home with clapboard painted white and green trim. The hip roof was made of tin and had big gable dormers. Outside our sleeping porch on the left of the front entrance was a night blooming Jasmine bush whose blossoms were still open and smelled wonderful.

For supper, we enjoyed the leftovers from Saturday's party. Essie warmed them up for us and then left to go home and be with her family. Lizzie and I did the dishes for her. At some point, Papa said we better get a good night's sleep because we would be going to school in Ocoee in the morning. He'd take us there in his car and we could walk to the dairy after school. We had a bunch of questions, but he just said, "You'll see."

When Janie came home all excited, the three of us went to our sleeping porch to talk. One of the girls she had met at church was Charlotte Anne Carrington, and Janie felt like she had known her all her life. The Carrington house was on an estate in Oakland, west of Winter Garden, where the wealthy folks lived. The mansion overlooked Lake Apopka, the biggest lake in the area, and they'd all gone out on a boat ride.

The Carrington's had company from out of town, a couple they knew from up north. Their son, whose name was Isaiah, was older than Janie. Charlotte Anne had known him for some time and told her that he'd been adopted by his folks. They visited often. In fact, they'd be back in Oakland for Christmas, and Isaiah had asked Janie if he could see her then, and she was thrilled and could hardly wait until he returned. He was a tall, good-looking young man with dark eyes and black hair. His features were very strong and his skin quite brown. Janie said that Charlotte Ann told her he was an Indian.

She told us all about him, but was scared to let on to Papa when he came to the door and said, "Lights out for tonight."

We whispered some more for a while, but I was tired from the long day and soon fell asleep.

When G'ma and her family arrived, Ocoee was an unincorporated town in West Orange County with a population of about 800 people. There were around 500 whites and between 250 and 300 blacks. The area included a number of businesses—a drug store, a grocery store, several saw mills, an automobile service station, and her grandfather's dairy. There were also two churches, separate schools for white and black children, and a post office. A dirt road, which later was paved with bricks, led to downtown Orlando, 15 miles away. Most of the residents worked in the citrus industry or in vegetable agriculture. The groves and farms ranged in size from three to a hundred or more acres, and the total community encompassed close to 40,000 acres.

On Monday morning, we got up at the crack of dawn and got ready for our first day of school. After breakfast Papa and Grandpa took us to the dairy so we'd know where to go afterwards. Papa was driving and turned left off the main road, crossed the cattle gap and traveled down the washboard dirt road for about half a mile. Along the way we saw Guernsey cows meandering and nibbling on the grass in a pasture fenced in with barbed wire. Up ahead was the dairy store, as it was called. It was a clapboard building all painted white, with a tin roof on top and two huge silos rising behind it where feed for the cows was kept. It had been a small saw mill house originally. Later on, Grandpa and Papa built additions to it, as the need arose, and they expanded their herd to close to seventy-five cows to meet the growing dairy needs of the customers in the surrounding area.

When we got there, we were surprised at the frenzy of activity. The cows needed to be milked, and Essie and Big Jim were there already getting started. Grandpa and Papa pitched in, too, and we did the best we could to stay out of their way.

When we were done and the milk was put up to chill, Essie and Jim walked to our house and Papa drove us to school in Ocoee, a mile and a half away. The building was called the "little red school house" because of the bright crimson color it was painted. I got put in third grade with fifteen students, and Miss Perkins was my teacher. Lizzie was in fourth grade. We both liked our school as much as anyone can like a new school, and that's all I have to say about that!

Our walk from school back to the dairy was fun and interesting. It was different every day. Some days the train would come through town hauling vegetables and citrus fruit and the engineer would wave and blow the horn for us. Other days we would visit with people on their porches that were talking and laughing or working. They would give us a big wave of goodbye as we left for the dairy. Occasionally the general store owner, Mr. Jones, would give us a piece of candy. Now, that was a real treat!

On the days it rained, if Papa wasn't too busy, he'd pick us up. In the late afternoon, the cows had to be milked again, but at a more leisurely pace, and we learned to become more useful and pitch in, carrying pails and containers and taking the cows back outside. Big Jim taught us how to milk them and, pretty soon, I got the hang of it.

Grandpa knew that the key to a successful dairy was the kind of cattle that furnished the milk. During the time he spent with Jake Summerlin, he'd learned that the breed was Guernsey cows, renowned for the rich flavor of their milk due to its high butterfat content. They have a docile disposition and are beautiful looking with their orange-red and white coats. I always liked spending time among these large, gentle creatures.

I thought it was also fun to be in the store and meet all the locals who came in to buy milk and share the latest gossip. The working people came themselves. The better off folks sent their black servants, and I'd overhear them sometimes, talking with Big Jim. That's when I realized that they knew a lot more about what was going on than their employers ever realized.

Janie didn't like working at the dairy store at all, so she got a job after finishing school minding the kids for the pastor and his wife. When that got boring, she asked Mrs. Maggie Malloy, who had a dress making business, if she needed any help, and Mrs. Malloy took her on as an apprentice seamstress. Fashioning dresses and hats made Janie real happy, and many a night she'd bring home the new clothes she was working on to show them off to us.

3

ESSIE, BIG JIM and LITTLE JIM

At home, we ate most of the daily family meals in the kitchen where Essie could serve all of us easily. Papa would tell us to help Essie by cleaning off the table after meals and putting the dishes in the washing area. He said, "I don't want helpless children to become helpless adults." What he didn't know was that we could not run the house without Essie there to tell us what to do.

Little Jim spent most of his time in the kitchen with Essie when he was at our homestead. The few times I talked with him I thought he didn't like me. He was very quiet and only answered my questions without offering any comments. But after a while, when we began to talk about school, work around the homestead, and his church, he opened up.

He told me that he lived around all grown up people and didn't get to spend time with other children much. I did find out that we were the same age and in the same grade at school even though we went to different schools in Ocoee. He said that his school was in an old Baptist Church right now, but there were rumors that a new school was going to be built, where all the Negro children would fit and even have room for some of the black youngsters of Winter Garden, too. He liked the idea of having a brand new school.

One afternoon when Little Jim, Lizzie and I wanted to stretch our legs, we took a walk down by the lake and climbed up an oak tree. From there, we could see as far as the end to the Northern Quarters on the other side, where Little Jim lived. Nearby there was a tree that had strange things hanging on it. Little Jim said it was a sausage tree and not ever to stand under it. Even though the shade is great, if one of the fruits fell, it could kill us. He also told us the dark red flowers only opened up at night.

We wanted to see it up close, but Old Blue, our porch hound, had followed us and started barking at squirrels, so we took him back to the house. Strange we never got to see that tree up close.

Little Jim thought his Mama was wonderful. "She cooks the best chit'lins in the quarters," he said smackin' his lips.

They'd sing church hymns together as they worked. The other day I heard them singing "The Old Rugged Cross." How great it sounded and I was surprised what a fine voice Little Jim had. He told me that Pastor Anthony, a guest pastor from Apopka, asked him to come to his church to sing.

Essie brought in a plate of fresh baked cookies and sweet milk from the dairy. I asked if we had any chocolate milk made from Papa's secret recipe. She said, "No, Mr. Ed sold all of the chocolate milk this morning."

The week of Thanksgiving we studied about Pilgrims, the Mayflower, and Indians in school. It must have been a really hard life with no houses and no roads. Before I knew it, Wednesday afternoon had come and gone. We were out of school until the following Monday. "Yippee!"

Earlier that week, Little Jim was snapping beans in the kitchen and Essie was peeling navel oranges to make marmalade. After I came in to help Little Jim, I noticed that she was singing the Juba song:

You sift-a the meal, you give me the husk.
You cook-a the bread, you give me the crust.
And then you Juba, you just Juba–

It was the same song as the children on the trip to Florida! So I asked her about it. She gave me a look like, "Do you really want to know?" By then she knew I had a curious mind and when I nodded eagerly, she said, "Lordie, child that is one of the oldest songs that the slaves used to communicate with one another, to talk about white folks so that white folks wouldn't know what was being said about them. Most times, slaves had to eat the scraps or leftovers of the food. Juba was, you know, just a jig to say their peace about conditions around them. Like 'Juba this and Juba that—Juba killed a yellow cat.' That meant mixed up food might make white folks sick, and they didn't care if it did. Juba helped get dark thoughts off black folks' brains and minds."

She stopped to see if I understood. I wanted to ask her some more about it, but then Big Jim came in. They got to talking about what she needed him to do to prepare the meal for that evening.

Big Jim had worked for Grandpa now for many years. He was a kind man. When a cow at the dairy was ready to give birth, he took care of her and after the calf was born made sure it was safe and eating.

When Grandma Mary Jane got sick a few years back, Jim and Essie came to work at the house full time. Essie worked inside doing the cooking, ironing and cleaning. Big Jim was a natural to do outside work. He would even sweep the sandy area with a home-made broom. I wanted to know why he did that and he said he could tell what type of critters was around the homestead by the tracks that were left. He showed me some of them—snakes, mice, coons and birds.

At the homestead, Big Jim kept the cattle gap repaired so the cows would not come in and eat the vegetables in the garden and the plants around the yard. Grandpa would laugh and say, "Big Jim is a Jack of all Trades!"

Big Jim would also help out Essie by gathering vegetables for the daily meal and moving furniture in the house when she cleaned. They were a real team, and now that all of us had moved in with Grandpa I hoped they would stay on.

Grandpa told us that Essie had worked for the governor of South Carolina's wife before moving to Florida. She would iron Grandma's bed sheets and spray them with lavender water before putting them back on the bed. One time while Grandma was bedridden, she even made a bed cap for her from lace that she had tatted, just to make her feel better.

Essie was a great cook and would serve food we all liked. She would ask what our favorites were. Every time she asked, I said, "Fried chicken with little biscuits, cut with a small can and her home-made marmalade."

After a great meal, Grandpa would say, "Mighty good eatin' Essie," and she'd reward him with a great big smile.

Essie knew how to set the table just so to make it pretty. She would use a small crystal vase or sometimes a jar with some flowers out of the yard in the center of the table. Her favorites were blue plumbago.

She and Big Jim had their own house and land in the Methodist Quarters north of Ocoee. Essie's family lived with them and took care of the farm and got Little Jim off to school. I remember when I said my prayers thinking how lucky we were to have Essie and Big Jim come to our house every day.

One night after supper I joined Big Jim on the front porch. He was sitting there smoking a cigarette. I asked him when he'd come to Central Florida, and he said he caught a wagon that was heading south in 1890. When I said, "Tell me more," he looked at me, checking out if I really wanted to hear his story and decided I did.

He started, "There was a bunch of us young workers from Travelers Rest, South Carolina. We were all looking to get us some land. Valentine was half Cherokee Indian and half Negro, so traveling with him was easier. He was light skinned and could go into general stores and diners for food and sup-plies without raising a fuss. He could read and write his name, which helped when haggling with store keepers over feed for the mules.

Also with us were Mose Norman and July Perry. They were older than the rest of us and had ambitions. I stopped when they stopped and all four of us wound up in Ocoee. The land here was the richest dirt I've ever seen. There is plenty of rain in the spring and summer with dry and cool winters—not cold. All around are these beautiful small lakes to fish in. Lake Apopka in South Apopka, about two miles to the west has lots of fish, too. It was a perfect place to farm and raise my family.

I was just a young kid and happy with my homestead and land, enough to grow sweet potatoes and corn and vegetables to live on. But Mose and July wanted more and bought more land over time, including an orange grove. It was just after the big freeze which killed all the oranges and destroyed a lot of trees. One of the small farmers who'd lost his whole crop and couldn't wait out the five years it takes to grow new trees sold his place to July and Mose, did it on the quiet."

I was surprised. "They sound like important people, but I haven't heard of them."

"You haven't been here all that long," said Big Jim. "Mose is a friendly, likable sort. He would help with hog killing, barn building and just about anything people asked of him. He would arrive in his shiny car with candy for the kids. On Sundays he would drive to Stuckey to pick up the preacher and then after church dinner he would take him back home. People in the neighborhood liked being around Mose. Not long ago, someone offered him ten thousand dollars for his part of the orange grove. That is a lot of money, but Mose said he'd worked it long and hard, and didn't plan to sell any time soon.

July has been successful, too, and worked his way to the top of the labor market. He finds jobs for the blacks on the farms and groves owned by the white people in the area, from Oakland and Winter Garden all the way to Apopka and Eatonville, and he charges both the workers and the owners for the service. He is well respected by the blacks in his community, and they will work where he says to work. He got married a while back by Pastor Hurston, and he and Estelle have several children. He is also a deacon in our Baptist Church. July is a serious-minded fellow and can be a bit prickly at times. He has a truck for hauling and nothing happens in the black community without him having a hand in it. He is an important man now."

Then Jim lowered his voice and said, "Mose and July belong to the black Masons. They asked me to join. I didn't want to at first, but then I figured, why not?"

I didn't really know what he was talking about, except that Papa and Grandpa were Masons, too, and kept going to meetings at the Blue Moon Lodge at Apopka. When I asked them why it had that name, Grandpa said it was because the meetings were always held on or before the full moon, so that people who came from all around the area would find their way and wouldn't get lost on the way home.

When Jim started talking again, I paid attention because I wanted to hear what he had to say. "Essie came to Ocoee later with her family from South Carolina," he told me. "Her older sister, Louise, had already moved to Florida when her good friend, Mrs. Mary McLeod Bethune, accepted an offer to run the mission school in Palatka. Mrs. Bethune needed help with her young son, Albert, and got in touch with Louise and asked her to help. So Louise came to stay with Mrs. Bethune and followed her when she moved to Daytona Beach to start a school for black girls.

The first time I saw Essie I knew I was gonna' marry her. She was a sight for sore eyes.

It wasn't long after our marriage when she was pregnant with our baby. There was a doctor in town, Dr. Bigalow, who Randall Betsy's wife told us to go see. Mrs. Betsy said that he had delivered her babies. Dr. Bigelow took good care of Essie and Little Jim. Our son arrived healthy that summer."

Essie must have heard him talking about her because she came out on the porch, wiping her hands on her apron, and sat down next to him for a spell. The way Jim looked at her with his eyes melting reminded me of the way Papa had looked at Mama. I wondered if someone would ever look at me that way.

The Northern or Methodist Quarters where Big Jim and Essie lived was one of three residential areas in Ocoee. The other two were the Center of town and the Southern Quarters. The Northern Quarters started at Tullulah, now known as Silver Star Road, and went all the way up to Fullers Cross Road. Generally speaking, most of the blacks that lived in the Northern Quarters were land workers, but some to the west near the Apopka-Ocoee Road, like July Perry and Mose Norman, also owned land.

The Center of town was sandwiched between the Northern and Southern Quarters. It was occupied by mostly white folks, although there was an apartment building near the Christian Church where several black families lived. The Southern or Baptist Quarters encompassed a smaller area, which started at White Road and went south to Minorville. It was a smaller neighborhood of black families. Some owned land, but most rented and worked for white people in their homes as servants and caretakers of their children.

On a side note, Pastor Hurston who married July and Estelle Perry was a Baptist preacher in Eatonville and the father of Zora Neale Hurston, who became one of the most important black women journalists and writers in the United States.

4

DARK CLOUDS
on the HORIZON

It was a year after G'ma traveled to Ocoee that World War I broke out in Europe. Because America was not involved for some time, it didn't have much of an impact on Central Florida. To be sure, there were occasional articles in newspapers that upset people and had them talking about this battle or that. The sinking of the Lusitania, a passenger ship torpedoed off the coast of Ireland by German U-boats in May of 1915, caused an international outcry. Altogether, 1,201 lives were lost, among them many women and children, and 128 Americans. But after Germany promised to stop its unrestricted submarine warfare, calls for U.S. intervention died down quickly. At that time America was still a solidly isolationist country.

For G'ma, far from European shores, where the Great War had descended into the brutal carnage and stalemate of trench warfare, a different kind of conflict invaded her home. It all started on February 8, 1915, with the premiere of D. W. Griffith's movie, *The Birth of a Nation*, which dealt with the post-Civil War era in the South and the rise of the Ku Klux Klan.

૭

In February, Judge Brownley, a retired judge living in Oakland, and his wife were invited by President Woodrow Wilson to attend a special showing of *The Birth of a Nation* in Washington, D.C. the following month. It would be the first moving picture ever shown at the White House and being asked to go was a great honor. Naturally, Mrs. Brownley wanted a special gown for the occasion, but when she asked her dressmaker, Maggie Malloy, she put the poor woman in a real quandary! Maggie didn't know how to tat lace, and Mrs. Brownley wanted lots of it. Fortunately, Maggie's servant, Pearl Blackshear, was a neighbor of our Essie and knew that she could do it. As a young girl in South Carolina, Essie had worked for the governor's wife and, among other skills, had learned how to hand tat lace. When Maggie heard about her, she hightailed to Ocoee and hired Essie on the spot.

Essie told Grandpa about it and he gave her permission to take the time she needed. After all, the whole area felt proud that the judge and his wife had been invited to the White House. For the next two weeks, Essie worked on that dress every spare minute, day and night. We all pitched in and took over as many of her chores and responsibilities as we could, even Janie. When the dress was finished, Essie showed it to us. It was a beautiful gown with lace everywhere. Essie had done a splendid job and Mrs. Brownley was very pleased.

Naturally I wanted to know what all the hullabaloo was about, so I asked Papa on the way to school one day. He didn't know a lot, but he told Lizzie and me what he'd read in the Orlando paper, that the movie told the story of the founding of the Ku Klux Klan after the Civil War.

That didn't mean anything to me at the time, but when the Brownleys came back from their trip, they were all excited about meeting President Wilson and having everyone say what a beautiful gown Mrs. Brownley was wearing. They spoke in glowing terms about the movie, although it lasted for more than three hours with an intermission! Janie heard from her friend Charlotte Anne that Judge Brownley said that every true Southerner should go see it.

I don't think Essie knew that she was working on a dress for someone to wear to that KKK movie! Of course, at the time, none of us knew how bad things would get because of that picture.

The Birth of a Nation was based on the novel and play *The Clansman* by Thomas Dixon Jr., a classmate of Woodrow Wilson at John Hopkins University. Part I dealt with the Civil War, President Lincoln's assassination, and the harsh punishment inflicted on the South by carpetbaggers during Reconstruction. In Part II, a half-crazed mulatto becomes Lieutenant Governor of South Carolina. During the election whites are disenfranchised by black militias and black voters stuffing the ballot boxes. One of the white men in the film starts the Ku Klux Klan, which hunts down a black, would-be rapist of a white woman and lynches him. Later, he and his fellow clansmen ride to the rescue of another white damsel in distress. The scene looks like the cavalry or knights in shining armor winning the day against "savage" Indians or greedy, evil nobles, which has become a staple in so many Hollywood movies ever since.

The epic battle scenes, thrilling chases, and melodrama amazed audiences. They'd never seen anything like it, and many responded with tears, cheers, and spontaneous applause. But there were also protests in a number of northern cities against the movies blatant racist message. The Birth of a Nation was greeted with riots in Boston,

Philadelphia and other major cities. In Lafayette, Indiana, after he saw the film, a white man murdered a black teenager. White gangs attacked blacks in a number of places throughout the United States. And while the mayors of northern cities, like Chicago, Denver, Pittsburgh, and St. Louis, banned or censored the film, worried that it would inflame racial prejudice, in the South, it was welcomed with open arms.

President Wilson after seeing the film was reported to have said, "It is like writing history with lightning and my only regret is that it is all terribly true." However, it is just as likely that Thomas Dixon made that up since he was tirelessly publicizing the film. Dixon went so far as to promote it as "Federally Endorsed."

After the controversy grew, the President did write that he disapproved of the "unfortunate production." But a quote from his book, History of the American People, written when he was a Princeton University professor and used in the film, suggests otherwise:

> The white men were roused by a mere instinct of self-preservation—until at last there had sprung into existence a great Ku Klux Klan, a veritable empire of the South, to protect the Southern country.

The glorification of the Ku Klux Klan in D. W. Griffith's picture inspired a new generation of white Southerners. In November of 1915, William J. Simmons and 14 other "charter members" refounded the Klan in a ceremony at Stone Mountain in Georgia. They reaffirmed the principles of the original, post-Civil War Klan: America first, white supremacy, separation of church and state, and chastity of womanhood. At their inaugural ceremony, they also started the practice of burning a cross, which had not been part of Klan activities during Reconstruction.

The Birth of a Nation was the highest grossing movie until another Civil War epic, Gone with the Wind, replaced it. And, the Ku Klux Klan used it as a recruitment tool into the 1970s!

I don't think G'ma ever saw *The Birth of a Nation*, although she heard about it (there were showings in Orlando and Jacksonville). Her own experiences of the Klan before the massacre were gentler and took the form of adolescent adventures.

O ne Saturday night, we had a party at our house with lots of neighbors attending. There was a fiddler after the meal and some people started to dance, with Janie leading the way. Lizzie and I were watching, feeling left out, when Ned came over and said he wanted us to come with him. We decided to join him and walked around Starke Lake. Then we took a left and hiked through an abandoned orange grove for a while. The oranges lying all over the ground made for a squishy walk. The place belonged to Mrs. Julia Ascot whose husband died suddenly. When she moved with her daughter to Atlanta to be close to her relatives, it fell into disrepair.

We finally got to a pump house that looked like a run-down, old shack and peeked inside through a smudge covered window. The moonlight fell on a white robe hanging on a wall inside. The door was catawampus, so we squeezed through a crack. Looking at the robe more closely, we realized that it belonged to the KKK. It was made of cotton and it had a hood with holes for eyes and a pointy top. Lying on a box nearby was a poster about a KKK rally and some KKK calling cards, as well as a sheet of paper with the rules for being a KKK member. I felt like a fist was tightening in my chest. Being inside that shack was scary enough, but not nearly as scary as when Ned put on the hood and came after us with arms raised and moaning like a ghost. Lizzie and I screamed.

In the silence that followed we heard a noise outside. Not knowing what it was, we hurried out of the pump house and ran as fast as we could back to Starke Lake. Even Ned looked worried. He said, "Don't you tell anyone what we found!"

We went back to our yard where the dancing was still going on and felt safe. The guests left about 10 p.m. and the house was finally quiet. When we went to bed, I asked Lizzie if she'd been afraid, and she whispered, "What do you think?" That's all we ever said about our trip to the pump house.

After the historic movie was shown, the KKK became more active. There were raids on blacks and people became more aware that the Klan was operating. In fact, Papa told a group of businessmen at our house that the Klan was experiencing one of the largest increases in membership in history. He said that "anybody who was somebody" was a member. It sounded to me like important people were involved and I knew where one of them kept his costume. According to one of the men at the meeting, West Orange County had the third oldest KKK group in the area.

I wondered if Papa and Grandpa belonged to the Klan, too. Is that why they went to their meetings at the Blue Moon Lodge at Apopka? I finally got up the courage to ask Papa, and he was startled at first. But then he smiled and said, "No, it's a different group called the Masons." When I asked, "What are they, bricklayers?" he laughed and replied, "No. It's a group of people dedicated to helping one another. They've been around for hundreds of years."

I must have looked confused, because he added, "I'll tell you more about it when you get older." I didn't understand what it meant, but I knew Big Jim was a black Mason, and I knew that he certainly didn't belong to the Klan. Little did I know then that most of the white Masons in the area were in the Klan, too.

On one of their travels, Papa and Grandpa picked up a radio! It was a huge thing that had a big battery. Papa charged the battery all week. He said that on Saturday night we could hear the Grand Ol' Opry straight from Nashville, Tennessee. He said we would invite some of our friends and neighbors over for supper and a candy pull, and listen to the radio. We were so thrilled helping Essie and Little Jim all week to prepare the food. Every time we would go past the radio we would get excited all over again.

Saturday finally came and during the afternoon people began to arrive with food and sugar cane molasses to make candy. Just when I was wondering if Ned would come, sure enough, he walked into our backyard with his mom, dad and sisters, and I was glad to see him.

He came over to us and said, "There is a full moon to-night!"

I replied, "What does that matter?"

He acted all mysterious. "Just you wait and see."

After a supper of venison, cornbread, string beans, grits and buttermilk biscuits—my favorite—it was time for the candy pull. Essie had cooked the molasses down to a small ball of paste and it was cool by now. We pulled it from both ends for a long time, folding it over and pulling again repeatedly until it was shiny and a fine delicacy. Then Papa cut it and we all ate the candy. What a treat!

It was almost time for the radio when Ned took me aside and said, "Let's go. You and your sister. And bring the dog." We went out on the porch and Ned told us that on the other side of Starke Lake the KKK was having a rally "Let's go and see what it looks like," he said, his eyes glowing with excitement.

I was scared, but wasn't going to let Ned see that or go without me, so I put Old Blue on a leash and followed him. Lizzie came along reluctantly.

Old Blue, our porch hound, had big sad eyes and huge ears that flopped when he walked. To hear him yelp and howl and start running with ears flying was too funny! He weighed about the same as me and was low to the ground and stubborn. When he made up his mind to go in one direction, there was nothing I could do to stop him, but for now he was on his best behavior.

We started out through the woods with Ned in the lead. It wasn't long until we saw light through the pine trees. It was bonfires burning. We sneaked closer and hid behind the palmettos and prickly pears. There were a bunch of people in white robes and hoods mingling about. Two of them came with a cross, stood it up, braced it and set it afire. Then two more hooded figures on horseback rode up to the cross on both sides, and all the others cheered and clapped.

Ned whispered, "Go to the left and wait until I holler. I'll meet you back at the front porch of your house, and don't get caught!" Then he disappeared into the bushes to the right.

Lizzie and I were too frightened to move and kept shooting glances at the fires. Suddenly we heard "W-o-o-o-o," from nearby. It was a high-pitched, blood-curdling yowl—Ned! So I cupped my hands around my mouth and wailed, "W-o-o-o-o." Then Lizzie joined in, "W-o-o-o-o!" and Old Blue started yelping and howling. He broke away from the leash and took off into the woods. The Klansmen looked confused and started to scatter heading in all directions.

We ran in the opposite direction as fast as we could. I felt the thorns from the prickly pears lashing my legs, but didn't care. When we got back to our porch, Old Blue was already there, thank goodness. Ned returned too, unharmed, and all three of us sat on the porch, trying to recover our breath. We didn't say a word to each other, but Lizzie's and Ned's faces were glowing.

Papa came out of the house and asked why we weren't there to hear the show. We said Old Blue got away and we had to chase him down in the woods. Papa gave us an odd look and said, "Another time then." We nodded eagerly. We'd already had our show!

Soon after the refounding of the Ku Klux Klan in Georgia, it grew and proliferated throughout the South, finding especially fertile soil in the Sunshine State. The early Klan activities were centered in Jacksonville, Miami and Central Florida. The third branch in the State, formed under the name Swamp Fire #3, was organized in Winter Garden in the spring of 1920. Next door neighbors in Ocoee and other surrounding communities, like Apopka and Orlando, held associate memberships. Estimates suggest that, at the time, as many as 90 percent of the area's law enforcement officers, judges, public servants, lawyers and railroad employees belonged to the KKK.

A good number of the participants in the Klan were also Free Masons. So many, in fact, that some newspapers in the 1920s claimed that the KKK was a branch of Free Masonry. There certainly are many Masonic overtones in the Klan—the emphasis on ritual, uniforms and disguise, and above all, the demands for secrecy. Whatever the case might be, a large number of the actors in the story of the Ocoee massacre were both Klansmen and Masons.

KEEPING THE PEACE

The election of Woodrow Wilson for a second term proceeded in 1916 with little controversy. "He kept us out of war," was his popular campaign slogan, meaning the great conflict in Europe and the Mexican Revolution. Everyone was happy about that, and in Florida whites and the few black voters who could afford to pay the poll tax, among them July Perry and Mose Norman, cast their ballots for him. Still, the "Schoolmaster from Princeton" won only a narrow victory nationwide, raising Republican hopes for 1920.

According to G'ma's journal, the most significant events in the Kambel's family life during that time were social in nature and concerned her older sister's efforts to find herself a suitable beau. Through her friendship with Charlotte Ann Carrington, Janie had entrée into the parties and dances of the area's upper crust, including big affairs at the newly built West Orange Country Club on John's Lake.

Charlotte Ann's father had come to Florida with his family because he'd known Charles Mather-Smith, a fellow manufacturer, in Chicago, who had retired here before him with his young wife, Grace. She was a former actress

47

and had a lot of spirit. When she and Charles first arrived in Orlando, they found the country club there too straight-laced and conservative for their taste. So they moved to Oakland and built a large mansion on Lake Apopka and founded their own club. Grace made sure the social calendar remained full and invited people from all over Central Florida. After visiting with the Mather-Smiths, Mr. Carrington, a devoted family man, had decided to retire to Oakland as well. That's when he built the large estate nearby called Oak Hill which overlooked Lake Apopka and adjoined the Mather-Smith's home.

With Christmas just around the corner, Janie was getting more excited about being invited to the party at the country club. One afternoon I saw her on our sleeping porch, hemming a dress to wear when Isaiah Winston came back to Oakland. She and Isaiah had gotten closer each year he'd visited with his family, and now that she was about to turn eighteen, she had her hopes up that he would propose to her.

Janie and Charlotte Ann would go over to the country club every chance they got to help with decorations and plans for the big Christmas party. They'd paint Magnolia leaves gold and drape them around the fire places and stairs, they'd put citrus fruit spiked with whole cloves and dusted with cinnamon throughout the club, and they'd festoon Florida holly that had such beautiful red berries at this time of year.

Janie told us that Mrs. Mather-Smith was always very nice to them, but she was very particular and demanding because she wanted to have everything decorated just so.

One afternoon, when none of the local stores had the kind of ribbons she wanted, she got in her car to drive to Orlando to go shopping. She tore down Highway 12 through Ocoee and the police stopped her for speeding. When the officer wrote out a ticket for ten dollars, she handed him a twenty-dollar bill, gave him her sweetest smile, and said, "Keep the change, because I'll be back through here soon, flying like a bat out of hell."

Janie told us that when all the decorating was done, it looked very beautiful. She was on pins and needles knowing Isaiah and Mr. and Mrs. Winston would be there soon coming by train. Mrs. Winston was a literary woman called a bluestocking and would perform a poetry reading at the party. Lizzie didn't care much about that kind of thing, but I wished I could be there and hung on Janie's every word. At some point, she told us that Mrs. Winston had brought another lady with her who would also read a poem or two. Her name was Victoria Crosswell. She had very dark hair and eyes, and tanned skin, and everyone said that she was Italian.

The night of the party arrived and Janie was so excited to see Isaiah she could hardly wait for Papa and Grandpa to drive her to Oakland and the country club. We figured she must have had a good time because, when she came home, her face was all aglow. We were eager to hear all about the party and Janie was happy to tell us. When she saw Isaiah, he quickly took her hand and she felt so comfortable, and they laughed and talked for a while. Lizzie and I rolled our eyes. Isaiah brought a Goo-Goo candy to her. She had never tasted anything like it and loved it. They went inside to dance and enjoy the food. What a wonderful party with Isaiah there. He took her hand again and kissed it, and that was wonderful. Lizzie and I rolled our eyes again.

The poetry performances were very well received. Everyone applauded but I could tell Janie was bored. Afterwards, one of the men wanted to take Victoria to Mel's Jook Joint. They and another couple got into his car and left the club. About thirty minutes later they returned upset, saying Victoria wasn't able to go into the Jook because no one believed her when she said she was Italian. The owners and the bar patrons had laughed and said, "Yeah, Eye-talian! Don't look like no Eye-talian I've ever seen. Looks mulatto to me."

It took a while for Mrs. Mather-Smith, Charlotte Ann's mom and Mrs. Winston to calm things down, but after a few dances, everyone was happy again. Janie said it was a "fine affair."

The New Year's Eve party was fun, too, with a small dance orchestra and spiced fruit punch, but we didn't hear about any of it until the next day when Janie was more matter-of-fact about it. She said Isaiah didn't propose to her as she hoped he would, but he'd done the next best thing. Around midnight, he had taken her off to one side of the porch overlooking the lake and said, rather formally, "I love you, Janie, but I want to wait until you're eighteen. If you'll have me I will then, I will go see your dad and ask for your hand." And then it was midnight and 1917 and he kissed her.

A week later Isaiah went back up north with his parents and Victoria Crosswell. Janie saw him off at the railroad station. When she came back to the house, she was forlorn for a week, and nothing we said or did cheered her up.

Not even the news that Little Jim was going to take part in a singing contest made her smile. When his voice broke and he no longer could sing soprano, everyone worried that he wouldn't be able to carry on as before, but in no time he became a fine baritone. He developed such a reputation that he was invited to enter the Orange County Black Gospel Sing sponsored by the local African Methodist Episcopal churches. The winner would go to the AME church in Daytona Beach for the State competition. I was so thrilled for him that the next morning, when Essie was making our breakfast, I asked her, "Do you think I can go to the sing?"

My request startled her and she quickly said, "Miss Georgia, you know your Papa couldn't let you go with us to a black church."

I wasn't ready to give up and quipped, "Well it's a house of God isn't it? The Good Book says that God looks at your heart not your skin color."

Essie replied seriously, "That is true, but unfortunately we have to deal with the people on this Earth, and they would make sure none of us even got to the sing."

I knew she was right and hung my head and went back to my room for a while. But I got over it in no time. If I couldn't go, I could still be happy for Little Jim and keep my fingers crossed that he would win.

For the next two weeks, Little Jim spent all his spare time practicing his songs. He even sang while he was doing his chores. His grandmother and Essie had decided, he should sing "The Old Rugged Cross" and, of course, Mr. Kambel's selection "It Is Well with My Soul."

Everyone at the homestead loved to hear him practice. It seemed to bring a new peace to the house. I thought to myself, "The right songs and prayers can make a difference."

Big Jim asked Mose Norman if he would drive Little Jim and the family to the Apopka AME Church for the Sunday sing. Mose Norman was happy to oblige, delighted to be able to show off his shiny car at such a special event. July and Estelle Perry with their children attended, too, to encourage Little Jim.

We went to our church, and I prayed that Little Jim would win. For the rest of the day, we were on pins and needles. On Monday morning we were all up early and waiting for Essie and the news about what happened at the sing. We gathered on the front porch and when we saw the big smile on Essie's face and the spring in her step, we knew it must be good news!

Grandpa said, "Come on, Essie, tell us all about it!"

She said, "Mr. Kambel, just let me get in the house."

Then she told us the story. The church was packed with people standing in the back. There were thirty singers and each one got to sing two hymns. There were even a couple of gospel groups. They were all good. Little Jim was on the schedule in the afternoon and when he sang "It Is Well with My Soul," you could hear a pin drop. After he finished the congregation stood, many with tears in their eyes, and applauded. The same thing happened with "The Old Rugged Cross." A few more individuals sang, and one more group, before it was over. The judges conferred for some time and gave first prize to one of the gospel groups.

We were disappointed and confused until Essie continued, "And they awarded the first runner-up in the Black Orange County Gospel Sing to James Booker Edwards!"

It was a big deal for a twelve-year-old boy to come in second place. When Little Jim arrived at our house after school, we welcomed him with cheers. I was so happy for him. I gave him a hug and said, "I knew you could do it!"

Normally shy, he broke out in a big grin and seemed to grow several inches.

HEARTBREAK

But such joyous moments were few and far between. For G'ma and her family, the bloody war in Europe came home all too soon. In early 1917, the German admiralty declared unrestricted submarine warfare and sank American passenger ships indiscriminately.

On April 2, President Wilson, the man who'd kept America out of war, went before a joint session of Congress and asked for a war resolution against Germany to make the world "safe for democracy." Four days later Congress complied. In May, the United States passed the Selective Service Act, allowing the federal government to draft men into the armed forces, and by the beginning of July, the first wave of American soldiers arrived in Europe.

In Florida, the call to arms to fight "the Huns" was greeted with great fanfare and patriotic fervor. Both white and black young men signed up in droves for what was called then "the American Expeditionary Force." For African Americans, it was not just a matter of pride, but an opportunity to show themselves as good citizens. Both black and white soldiers going off to war received rousing send offs at the railroad stations by their respective communities. In fact, black recruits and volunteers made up over half of the state's soldiers.

Soon there was a backlash among the powerful growers and plantation owners. They liked having a ready supply of cheap labor and felt that the out flux of so many field laborers would cripple agriculture and cut into their profits. When they complained about the U.S. Employment Service recruiting workers for government defense plants, the federal government acquiesced and stopped its efforts even though it impeded the war effort.

While Ocoee and the surrounding communities sent their share of black and white young men off to war, July Perry and Mose Norman managed to find ways to keep the local economy going. No doubt the resentment on the part of white growers increased, since the two labor brokers made sure their groves and fields came first. But there were still plenty of people willing to do a day's work for low wages, and although the war effort meant everyone had to tighten their belts, life went on pretty much as before.

The minister in church preached fire and brimstone against the Germans and told us that we all had to do our part and to join the effort to defeat the Huns. He was a rousing speaker, and got us all excited. Grandpa said he wished he were younger, so he could go off and fight for our country.

Several boys and young men from Oakland, Winter Garden and Ocoee signed up, including Hoseah Atkins, Leo Borgard, Elmer McDaniel, and Frank Weaver. Ned talked big about lying about his age so he could go with them, but I knew it was just a lot of blustery hot air. One afternoon, Big Jim told us that fifteen black men from the Methodist Quarters and three from the southern part of town joined up with the U.S. Army. He and Essie, along with their proud folks and neighbors from the black community, went down to the train station to see them off. I wanted to go, too, but Essie said it would be better if I stayed home.

In July, Janie received a letter from Isaiah saying that he had enlisted in the army "to do what's right" and was about to ship out for England. He told her that he would always love her and to keep thinking of him.

Janie started to pray more fervently at church and at night before we went to bed, asking God to keep Isaiah safe. She'd get down on her knees and put his letter in front of her and pray. Then she'd kiss the letter and put it in a drawer in her dresser.

Every day, she'd be out in front of our house waiting for the mailman to arrive, hoping for a letter from Isaiah, and she was rewarded three months later when a letter came from England. When she read that he was all right and how much he missed her, she started to cry tears of sadness and joy that he was safe and covered the paper he had written on with kisses.

Another letter arrived around Christmas, the best present she could have wished for. Not much else happened over the holiday, except the Winston's came down to visit the Carrington's and went out of their way to meet up with Janie, treating her very much like a future daughter-in-law and telling her how happy she and Isaiah would be together.

In February, yet another letter came, this time from France. It had traveled to England and then by ship to New York and from there by train to Florida. Janie was thrilled and added it to her collection for her prayers. What we didn't know was that, by the time we received the letter, Isaiah was already gone, killed in the Battle of Cambria.

We found out about it in early March. I was in the kitchen helping Essie prepare the meal when we heard an unearthly screaming. It sounded like a wounded animal and it raised the hair on my neck. By the time we rushed to the living room it had stopped and we found Janie kneeling and banging her head on the floor. An open letter lay nearby.

Lizzie, Little Jim and I were rooted to the spot, not knowing what to do. But Essie went into action. She wrapped her arms around Janie and held on tight even though Janie kept trying to shake her off. Her eyes were wild, darting all over the place, and blood was pouring from her forehead. Essie hunkered down next to Janie and got her to sit. Cradling her in her arms, Essie squeezed her tight and kept talking to her like a little girl, murmuring, "There, there," until Janie suddenly stopped fighting and went all limp. The moan that escaped from her lips was almost as bad as the screams.

By then Grandpa and Papa had arrived, but Essie shooed them from the room with a fierce glance.

When Janie started to sob quietly, Essie kept saying, "Its okay, honey, its okay," over and over.

Lizzie and I stood by as helpless witnesses. I felt bad for Janie but also glad that we had Essie to help. I don't know how we would have managed without her.

After a while, Essie got to her feet and helped Janie up. With her arms wrapped around her, holding her close, she took Janie to our sleeping porch and put her to bed. She got a moist towel to still the quelling cut on her forehead and stayed by her side until Janie fell asleep. Then she told us to keep her company while she went off to talk to Papa and Grandpa.

I got Mama's crocheted counterpane from the chest of drawers and gently covered Janie up. It always made me feel better when I used Mama's counterpane and I hoped it would help Janie, too.

Janie stayed in bed for several days and we tiptoed around her when we went to bed at night and woke in the morning. She didn't say a word for three days, and even after she finally got up and joined the rest of us, she seemed like someone raised from the dead.

She often had a faraway look in her eyes. Questions and comments from us would shake her out of her reverie for a while. Essie kept talking to her as if nothing had happened and encouraged us to do the same. Papa and Grandpa let her be, figuring that it would take time and, in a way, they were right.

After a few months, Janie seemed to recover, but she wasn't the same as before. The corners of her mouth were drawn tighter and there was no light in her eyes when she smiled. It was like she no longer believed in happiness. The great love of her life had died, and she didn't believe she could have another. She became more critical, calling many of the things we did childish, and she started to keep her distance from Essie. Time may have healed her, but as far as I could tell, it only put a scab on the wound.

AFTER THE WAR

While World War I brought anguish to G'ma's home, it ended with a sense of victory for our side. America had been "the savior of the world" and peace was restored. Only in retrospect do we know that it was a fantasy and how badly things turned out. There would be financial turmoil and economic ruin in Europe, the Russian Revolution, and the rise of Fascism in Italy and Germany. The Treaty of Versailles, in which the victorious nations made draconian reparation demands over vanquished Germany, all but ensured another horrific world war 20 years later.

It was hard seeing Janie being so sad all the time. No one knew how to cheer her up. Grandpa and Papa tried in their gruff ways, but didn't get anywhere, and we were too young. Essie was the only one who could have, but Janie avoided her. Someone else might have been grateful, but for Janie it was as if Essie taking care of her during her breakdown had shamed her, and she didn't want to be reminded of a black maid seeing her so vulnerable.

The only thing that helped was her job. After she'd graduated from the eighth grade at the top of her class, Papa hadn't let her go to Orlando to board at a finishing school, and working at the dairy was out of the question for her. Around that time the pastor's wife, Louise Marie Evans, had twin girls, and Janie would watch them during the day and sometimes in the evening, so Mrs. Evans could be more help to her husband with the growing congregation. Taking care of the babies gave Janie something meaningful to do, and the pastor's wife ministered to her in a quiet way. That was before she started sewing for Mrs. Malloy.

Charlotte Ann wanted her to come out to some of her mom's parties and social events in Oakland and at the Mather-Smith's country club. Apparently, there were a lot of eligible young men who expressed an interest in her, but Janie refused all invitations, like a widow in mourning.

November 11, Armistice Day, came on a Monday. When we got to school, our teacher told us the war was over and dismissed us for the day. I don't know if I was happier at the news, or getting a day off school. As I walked to the dairy, churches were ringing their bells and people came out of their shops and houses and cheered and hugged one another.

We heard later that there was an even bigger ruckus in Orlando. The whistles from the Orlando Water and Light Company plant woke everyone up with their shrill blasts, a prearranged signal for the end of the war. People poured into the streets, laughing, crying, hooting and hollering, honking automobile horns, rattling tin cans, shooting guns into the air, and dancing with the nearest stranger. All the stores closed by proclamation from Mayor Giles, and blacks and whites together paraded spontaneously all over town singing patriotic songs. It was nothing like Orlando had ever seen.

There was one dark cloud that hung over the rejoicing. Janie got all upset again, retreated to her room and refused to come out for three days. We all pleaded with her, but to no avail. Both Lizzie and I were getting a little cross with her. We couldn't understand why she would be forlorn for so long. After all, she hadn't been that upset when Mama died, but Essie hushed us and said we were too young to understand.

Besides, there were other things to worry about. I had my hands full fending off Ned's unwanted attention. He was teasing me constantly since he ended up in my class at school. He would come by my desk and knock my papers off and laugh at me while I picked everything up one more time.

One day he left a folded paper in one of my books. I didn't know who it was from until I opened the whole paper and saw a pencil drawing of a man on horseback, dressed in full white KKK regalia with a pointed headpiece and cut outs for the glaring eyes. All the note said was, "BOO! Gotcha. N." It gave me cold chills all over my body. I knew then why Ned was such a terrible academic student because he spent his day drawing things to frighten others. I figured his dad must be a member of the Klan even though he was friendly with everyone at picnics and church functions.

At some point, Ned also told me that Langmeade, a mulatto carpenter, who owned land over on Kissimmee Avenue, had been beaten by the Klan for disagreeing with a white man on a job. Apparently, he thought he knew better how to put in windows for a new house and made no bones about it. On his way home, they took him, tied him to a tree, whipped him and hurt him badly. Ned didn't know if it was true, but word was that, for a while, Langmeade sat on a pillow everywhere he went.

By May, all of the soldiers had come back from the war. Our minister had the ones from our town stand up one Sunday and be recognized for their service to God and our country. When I asked Essie about the black soldiers from our area, she told me that the same thing happened in their church with a big barbecue afterward in celebration.

But the biggest jamboree happened in Orlando with a victory parade for all the white soldiers. A week before, Grandpa made an announcement at Sunday dinner that we'd be going. As we all knew, he had traveled to many of his Civil War reunions and always brought new medals back. He said we needed to get busy polishing them because he would wear them with his uniform in honor of the young World War I veterans. Except for Janie, who remained quiet, we all talked for a while and then Essie served her wonderful banana pudding for dessert.

I did my homework on Monday and then started polishing Grandpa's metals. It must have been quite some time since he'd gone to a reunion because they were all tarnished dark green and black, not shiny and bright. It took a while but I got them to sparkle, and Grandpa was pleased.

That Saturday all of us except Janie piled into the car and Papa drove the fifteen miles to Orlando. Grandpa looked magnificent in his gray Confederate uniform with the medals on his chest sparkling in the sun. On our way to the parade, we passed the Grand Theater where *Birth of a Nation* was playing at night to sell-out crowds. We took Grandpa to where the other Civil War veterans were gathering, and then Papa, Lizzie and I walked further down Pine Street to find a good spot to stand and watch. Along the way, we got little American flags.

The parade was wonderful, with a big marching band out front. Soldiers dressed in olive brown uniforms marched smartly past us, carrying banners and flags that fluttered in the wind. There was a bugle corps, too. A man standing next to us said it was an okay celebration, but nothing like the ruckus on Armistice Day a few months earlier.

We waved our little flags at the passing war veterans. I kept my eyes out for Grandpa and when I finally saw him, yelled out, "Hurray, Grandpa!" He heard and without missing a step turned his head toward us and saluted. I'd never felt prouder in my life up till then.

The soldiers who had fought in World War I were happy to return home, even if it meant coming back to places that seemed smaller and shrunken after what they had seen. Some of them were changed by the experience—it broadened their horizons in more ways than one—and they came back with new expectations of what their lives would be like.

That was especially true of African Americans who had fought in Europe and found a new sense of freedom and dignity "over there." True, they had encountered racism on the part of their white officers, who didn't think they could fight, but they had acquitted themselves splendidly in battles and earned the respect of many of their fellow white soldiers. After Armistice on November 11, 1918, grateful Parisians and French villagers, on whose behalf they had fought so bravely, treated them with gratitude, fascination and, above all, as equals. So they returned with an expectation that they would be rewarded for their patriotic service, that things would not be the same as before, and that Jim Crow would become a thing of the past.

Many sought to organize for better wages and civil rights, but the competition for jobs with returning white soldiers and the fear of Communism coming to the United States after the Russian Revolution, led to violent altercations. It didn't help that President Wilson branded the black soldiers who had served so courageously in Europe as Communist subversives and declared that "the American

Negro returning from abroad would be our greatest medium in conveying Bolshevism to America." During the Red Summer of 1919, there were race riots in more than three dozen cities across the United States. When blacks fought back against the mostly white attackers, blood flowed. In Chicago 38 people died—23 African Americans and 15 whites.

There were calls for emancipation and efforts to organize black labor in the growing fields and orange groves, and on the railroads throughout Florida. Although there was a growing movement and even some strikes, they did not meet with success. White farm owners got together and slashed daily wage rates in some counties. Police and other law enforcement officials assisted in the repression of workers by arresting strikers and union organizers.

Surprisingly, Ocoee with its large black community remained quiet and calm. True, there were rumblings and demonstrations in surrounding cities like Jacksonville, but July Perry and Mose Norman controlling the black labor market kept a lid on things. Any organizing for change took place without any public display in the quiet of people's homes.

It also helped that by 1919 Ocoee was a growing, prosperous village. It had electric lights, water works, a hotel and three houses of worship for the white population—an Episcopal Church having joined the Methodist and Christian Church. There was a drug store and a general store downtown, and daily automobile service connecting the area to Oakland, Winter Garden and Orlando. The construction of the first brick building, the Bank of Ocoee, inspired a special pride in the community and signaled a thriving economy.

Under such circumstances, the black community did well, too. Many of the residents living in the Methodist Quarters north of Tullulah were comfortably middle-class. At least 25 families owned their own homes. The same was true in the Southern Quarters.

Altogether there were more than 400 black inhabitants in Ocoee by then, nearly half of the population. Everyone seemed to be doing well. But there were undercurrents of trouble brewing, and they would soon reach the boiling point.

With the dairy growing, Papa and Grandpa realized they needed to hire additional workers, especially a good cowhand to round-up the cattle every morning for milking. They thought of David Douglas who was a skilled horseman and cattle roper. When Papa offered him the job, David said yes right away. He turned out to be an excellent employee who took much of the burden of dealing with the cows off Papa's shoulders so he could concentrate on the overall management of the dairy.

Papa soon realized that he needed additional help in the store, too, and would require a dependable, honest and well liked person. The one that came to mind was Sarah Tillison whose parents were suppliers of the dairy. When Mr. Tillison came to deliver his corn husks for the feed silos, Papa asked him if Sarah would be interested in running the dairy store.

The next morning Sarah came to the dairy, accompanied by her father and they worked out terms with Papa. So, all was set and Papa had two new capable employees to help with the needs of his fast-growing business. That wasn't all about David and Sarah. With them seeing each other every day romantic sparks began to fly and before we knew it there was a new couple in town. They would talk and laugh at work. Soon they started to go to different socials in the area.

As the herd of cows increased, we also needed more pasture land. Papa asked Grandpa what he thought about hiring men from July Perry to help clear some of the forested areas on our land. Grandpa figured that was a good idea and asked Essie to have July stop around the homestead the next day after supper to talk.

That Thursday night at 7 p.m. sharp, there was a knock on the back door. Essie came into the living room and said that July had come to talk to Papa and Grandpa.

Lizzie and I went to the kitchen window and peeked out. I'd seen July Perry from a distance once or twice before, but never up close. He appeared to be older than Papa and wore a dark brown jacket over a white, linen shirt. He was stocky, but not as tall or muscular as Big Jim. Although his eyes were hidden under a big, wide-brimmed hat, I noticed the determined set of his jaw and mouth.

I wanted to go out and meet him, but Papa said, "No, Georgia you have a spelling test to study for tomorrow."

So I watched as the three men walked down to the lake. July took his hat off and held it in his hand as they talked. He had short, curly dark hair. The three looked like three serious-minded men discussing business. I wondered why Essie didn't serve July a drink or something to eat.

Before long they reached a suitable agreement. Papa and Grandpa came back to the house without July. The following day, a crew of black men arrived at the dairy. For the next few weeks they worked from morning till sundown to clear out a large wooded section at the back of the property. It was hard going because they had to cut down all the shrubs and trees and take out the stumps, including all the saw palmetto, which had deep roots that clung to the soil and had to be dug out. But they did a good job, and Papa and Grandpa were very pleased.

There was one other matter to attend to. For a while Papa and Grandpa had been discussing selling the Overland

Touring Car and getting a new truck to help with milk and cheese deliveries and hauling the hay and other supplies. So Papa put the Overland out in front of the dairy with a for sale sign on it.

It wasn't there long when Captain Sims came by. He normally didn't pick up his dairy order himself—he had his Negro servant do that—but there he was. He said to Papa, "I see you've got your car up for sale."

Papa said, "Yes sir. She's a good one, but we need a truck for the dairy."

Captain Sims said, "I just might be interested in it for my son."

Papa told him it was a 1903 Overland Touring Car with a canvas roof and no side windows, only curtains. It was a popular model. In the early 1900s, the Overland Company sold more cars than Ford Motor Company. Well, Captain Sims looked under the hood and took it for a spin. When he returned, he looked satisfied and told Papa that he thought it would be perfect for his son. As the local dentist, he often had to make house calls. They haggled over the price for a while, and then settled on a firm offer. Now Papa could buy the new truck that he needed for the dairy.

I was sad to see it go. I loved that old car and cherished all the memories that I had of Mama and our trip coming to Florida.

8

WEDDING BELLS

What finally pulled Janie out of her blue funk was the arrival of a letter from Charlotte Ann. She was getting married in May and wanted Janie to be her maid of honor. She had been attending Mrs. Princeton's Finishing School for Young Ladies in Washington, D.C. and met her fiancé at one of the debutante balls. Captain Maynard "Duck" Duckworth was a West Point graduate and career Army man. He came from a distinguished Virginia family going all the way back to the American Revolution and had proposed to her with his grandmother's diamond engagement ring. Janie had known that they were getting serious, but the announcement of a spring wedding was a surprise and got her all excited. Charlotte Ann would be home after finishing school in late April and make sure to get everything ready for what promised to be the social event of the year. In the letter she also asked Janie if we, her sisters, who were invited to the wedding, too, would kindly help her mother in the meantime?

Well, no sooner had Janie put the letter down than she flew into action. She called on Mrs. Mather-Smith, who was planning the wedding for the Carrington's, and offered her assistance, which was graciously and gratefully accepted. The engraver had just finished the invitations, and they needed to be sent out to the guests. Many of them were coming from up north and needed at least six weeks to get ready and make their travel arrangements. Janie had good handwriting and would help with the task of getting them out in time.

She volunteered us to help Lena, Mrs. Carrington's maid. There was silver to be polished, windows to be cleaned, linens to be washed and ironed, and floors to be scoured and waxed. The gardener had his hands full, too, getting the yard ready for the reception. Lizzie and I went out to Oakland after school and on weekends and joined the whirlwind of activity. We were so pleased that Janie was happy again that we didn't mind the drudgery very much.

By the time the excited bride arrived, we were a month out from the wedding, and much remained to be done. Charlotte Ann told Janie that she wanted her bridesmaids, all five of them, to wear dresses of pink organdy, to go with all the beautiful azaleas around the yard, and sent her to a dressmaker in Orlando to be fitted. Her family was paying for it. Lizzie and I would have to fend for ourselves, however, to get our formals for the reception afterward.

That's when Lizzie put her foot down. She'd wear her Sunday's best to the church ceremony, but she wouldn't go to the reception, and that was that. Janie pleaded with her, but Lizzie was adamant. Wild horses couldn't drag her there. She'd rather stay home with Old Blue. Although she was a year older than me, she was still shy as a wall flower.

But I really wanted to go. Janie told me to talk to Essie since she was an excellent seamstress.

When I mentioned the wedding to her, Essie smiled and said, "I've already talked to your Papa about it. Come with me."

We went into his bedroom to Mama's hope chest and found a lovely lavender dress, with a scoop neckline and a flowing A-line skirt that Essie could use to make a formal. She'd tat some lace to add to the front for accent and make the sleeves coming over my shoulders into cap sleeves. I also found a lovely pair of matching shoes that I could wear with a bit of newspaper stuffed in the toes. How lucky I was to have all this.

Essie measured me then cut and sewed for a while. Then she fit me again and pinned the lace she had made down the front. When I looked in the mirror, I was amazed. I hardly recognized myself. I really looked pretty in the dress, even if I said so myself. Essie agreed that the light lavender was a great color with my dark hair and creamy complexion. "You know, Georgia, you have your Papa's big blue eyes," she commented, and I flushed with pleasure.

When I modeled the dress for the family for the first time, Lizzie went all pale and ran off into another room. But when Papa looked at me, tears came into his eyes. "You look so beautiful, darling," he said. "I wish your mama could see you, she would have loved it."

I gave him a big hug as tears streamed down my face, too.

During the last days before the wedding, Janie stayed at Charlotte Ann's house so she and the bride could go to the railroad station together and meet the trains bringing all the guests and cadets from up north and participate in the rehearsal and dinner. Mrs. Carrington had booked all the rooms in the Oakland Hotel for the out-of-towners. Janie also helped Charlotte Ann keep track of all the gifts that kept arriving.

Saturday late morning, Papa, Grandpa, Lizzie and I drove to the Oakland Presbyterian Church. Janie was already there, looking very beautiful in her pink organdy dress, and she introduced us to the groom's party. Retired Colonel Duckworth and his wife, and General and Mrs. Hester Temple, the parents of the best man, all seemed very distinguished. Duck's friend and best man, Jackson Temple from Virginia, and a number of West Point cadets surrounded the groom, who looked handsome in his dress uniform but kept pacing around nervously. Grandpa was wearing his confederate uniform. If any of the Yankee military men thought it was odd, none of them said so. In fact, they all had a fine time sharing war stories with him.

The ceremony was wonderful. When Charlotte Anne came walking down the aisle, there were gasps of pleasure all around. Her dress was embellished with hundreds of sparkling beads. The sleeves were long, the neck had a slight scoop with two more rows of beading, and the skirt flowed to the floor. The bouquet she carried was a cascade of orange blossoms and gardenias. It was the most magnificent dress I'd ever seen, and she looked like a fairy queen floating toward her betrothed. My very favorite part was when the cadets, standing at attention with their sabers drawn, made an arch for the bride and groom to walk through after the ceremony.

I liked the reception even better. The food tables were bountiful and the head table was heaped with crab cakes and the biggest shrimp I'd even seen, and a big crystal bowl filled with citrus punch and fresh fruit in the center. There was a five-piece orchestra playing dance music.

Janie danced with Duck's best man. She and Jackson made an even more handsome couple than the bride and groom, but no one would have dreamed of being as unkind as to point it out. When Ross Field, one of the cadets came up to me, bowed from the waist and asked me to dance, I was surprised and pleased. From the way he looked at me and held me in his arms, I could tell he wasn't just doing it because I was the younger sister of the maid of honor.

After a while, Mr. Carrington danced with Charlotte Ann to the song, "Daddy's Little Girl." Then he made a champagne toast to go with the cutting of the cake. I just sipped my champagne glass. After the delicious punch, it tasted tart, and I didn't understand what all the fuss was about.

I was happy to see Janie glow with pleasure from all the attention she got from the military visitors and the young men from the wealthy families in the area. One of them, Clayton Eugene Pike, asked her to dance several times. He was handsome in a way—tall, slender, with a tanned complexion, brown hair and green eyes. Janie obliged him once, but spent most her time with Jackson.

I sat on the veranda close to the lake to have some food and rest for a minute. Out of nowhere, I started to think about how Lizzie reacted when she saw me in the dress. Was she envious or upset because it reminded her of Mama?

I didn't get a chance to ponder any further, however, because Ross came and sat with me. He said, "I'm leaving early Monday morning for Chicago." Then he took my hand and kissed it. I blushed and we sat in silence for a while.

Soon it was time to bid the bride and groom good-bye. They were going to spend the night at the lake house. Janie had a basket of food for them and Jackson carried their suitcase to the car. Afterward, when he took Janie by the hand and they went out on the veranda, I noticed Eugene Pike, standing by the punch bowl, with his eyes ablaze and his jaw clenched very tightly. He definitely was jealous!

But I wasn't going to let his feelings spoil the evening for me. I danced some more with Ross until my feet hurt. Later, Jackson drove Janie and me home to Ocoee. I went inside first to give them some privacy but sneaked a look out the window and saw him kiss her good-night.

9

EUGENE

Charlotte Anne's wedding restored Janie's sunny disposition, especially because Eugene Pike started to pay her serious attention. He came to the dairy one afternoon the following week, dressed in a suit, when Janie was there, and asked if he could take her to a dance Saturday Night in Clarcona, which was about three miles north of Ocoee. When she checked with Papa to get his permission, he said it was fine. I guess he figured that any young man who gussied himself up for his daughter was all right.

That night, while they had their after-dinner cigars together in the sitting room, he asked Grandpa, "Do you know the Pike family very well?"

Grandpa said, "Sure do."

After he told him all he knew, Papa was even more pleased.

Saturday night came and Janie was all excited and ready for the dance. Eugene picked her up in his family's car, which impressed everybody, and they were off.

Well, it was only a couple of hours later when Janie came back into the house in a huff, saying some of Eugene's friends showed up and told him he had to leave the dance early and go to a special lodge meeting. He didn't want to, but they teased him until he said yes. Papa and Grandpa shared a look, as if they knew what that meant.

Several days later during recess at school, Ned in his irritating way motioned me over to the side of the building. He proceeded to tell me the latest tidbit! Eugene and his friends James and John had prearranged to meet with several "girls" at the Jook in Eatonville last Saturday Night after the Clarcona dance. "I heard that they had a wild time," Ned said. "For sure, that Eugene better watch it or he'll be have'n a black young'en before he knows it."

I didn't know what to do. If I told Janie, she'd probably say it's a lie. Besides, I didn't trust Ned to tell the truth about anything. He was such a trouble maker. So I kept quiet.

Eugene continued to court Janie like a gentleman with small presents and flowers, and took her to dances in the area and the movies in Orlando. Janie thought he was wonderful. Although he was slow talking, he seemed sure of himself. It didn't hurt that he came from a rich family that owned a lot of orange groves. They didn't have as much money as the Mather-Smiths, but they certainly were high up among the Ocoee elite.

The Pikes originally came from South Carolina. John Pike was a friend and Masonic brother of Captain Sims, who promised he would help him get started in the citrus industry. So John and his wife Margaret moved to Ocoee in 1890. Like July Perry, he took advantage of the big freeze that destroyed much of the orange crop and bought up groves from farmers who had fallen on hard times. He had a lot of money to spend and quickly became one of the largest landholders and growers in the area. Eugene was his only child and grew up privileged and groomed to take over the family business.

There is a statute of a man named Albert Pike in Washington, D.C. He was a brigadier general for the South during the Civil War, the only confederate soldier to be honored with a monument in the U.S. Capital. He was also an important Free Mason, as well as Sovereign Grand Commander of the Scottish Rites Southern Jurisdiction for 32 years. The organization sponsored and paid for the statue, which shows him in civilian dress as a Masonic leader, not a Confederate general.

John Pike always claimed that Albert Pike was an important ancestor of his. When Eugene was still a boy, his father took him on a special trip to Washington to see the statue and tell him all about it. It was almost like a pilgrimage to a family shrine, but there is no evidence that they were related.

At some point, Eugene came by the homestead and asked Papa if he could talk with him. Janie was in the backyard unsuspecting, but Lizzie and I listened from the porch because the window to the drawing room was open.

Eugene said, "Mr. Kambel, I know Janie and I have not been dating very long, but I love her and I want to ask for her hand in marriage."

There was a silence, and I imagined Papa looking him straight in the eyes. Then he asked, "Eugene, do you want to take care of her and spend the rest of your life with her?"

"Yes, sir," he said earnestly.

Papa thought for a moment and then said, "I know you can provide for her, but is Janie in love with you? If she is and wants to marry you, I'll be happy to give the two of you my blessing."

Lizzie and I sneaked out back and watched from behind a water barrel as Eugene came out of the house and went over to Janie who was in the big swing. He got down on one knee, took her hand, held out a lovely diamond ring, and said, "Will you marry me?"

Her eyes filled with tears and she whispered, "Yes."

As he put the ring on her finger, Lizzie and I crept back inside. Soon Janie came into the living room like she was gliding on air. "You won't believe what just happened," she exclaimed. "Clayton Eugene Pike asked me to marry him, and look at my beautiful diamond ring!"

We acted like we were surprised and oohed and aahed over the ring, but I had mixed feelings. I figured that Eugene would propose to Janie, but not this soon. Maybe he wanted to marry my sister after the gossip about him going to Eatonville, which he and his friends apparently visited regularly. I wondered again if I should tell Papa what I'd heard. But he and Grandpa treated Janie with kid gloves since Isaiah had been killed in the war. If I confronted Janie now, she would surely say it was a lie and I was just jealous. Sometimes I think all she cares about is his family's position, money, and land holdings.

Grandpa was returning from the lakefront where he had been fishing. When Janie ran to him, gave him a big hug and told him the news. He seemed shocked but quickly returned her embrace.

Janie put out her hand and said, "Look at my ring. Isn't it beautiful?"

Grandpa nodded and said, "That must have set him back some."

Just then, Papa came into the room and Janie rushed to him. "Oh, Papa, Eugene asked me to marry him, but you know that already, don't you?"

Papa replied, "Yes, Janie. I hope the two of you will be very happy."

Later that day Eugene returned to get Janie so they could tell his parents the good news. The Pike's were delighted and Mr. Pike said he'd announce their engagement at church the next day. He added, "Janie, bring your family to the service. Then it will be official, and the news will spread like wild fire through the community."

And so it did. Everyone wanted to know when they would be "tying the knot." Janie was so excited with all the attention she was getting. She and Eugene decided to be married at the Ocoee Christian Church, but they did not set a date right away.

From that point on, Janie spent time at her beau's home, and he came over for dinner to our house. Eugene was always well-mannered and courteous to Lizzie and me, but he treated Essie and Big Jim, who were family as far as I was concerned, as if they didn't exist.

One time he and Papa got into a conversation about the problems the Pikes were having with July Perry and Mose Norman as labor brokers. "They're hogging their best pickers for their own groves, and we have to pay them for the workers they send us more than they're worth," he complained. It sounded like he was parroting something he'd heard at home. Papa said that he didn't have that problem at the dairy farm and changed the subject.

I went into the kitchen to help Essie clean up and heard her say to Big Jim, "Something ain't right with that boy. You better be careful around him."

When she saw me, she shot me a quick glance, as if she wondered what I heard.

I said, "I don't like him either. He's a spoiled brat!"

Essie looked surprised and a small smile formed around the corners of her mouth. From that point on, she became less guarded around me when talking about things going on in our community.

∽

POLITICS

Part of what was holding up the wedding plans was that 1920 was a presidential election year, and Janie and Eugene wanted to wait until after all the political excitement had died down.

In early June at their convention in Chicago, the Republicans nominated Ohio Senator Warren G. Harding as their party's standard bearer and Calvin Coolidge, governor of Massachusetts as his running mate. Harding's slogan and campaign promise after the upheavals following World War I was "Return to Normalcy." The Democrats countered later that month in San Francisco by putting Ohio's governor, James D. Cox on the ticket for president and Franklin D. Roosevelt, the Assistant Secretary of the Navy, as vice presidential candidate.

The upcoming election was on everyone's mind and came up in conversations everywhere. But what had everyone talking were women suffrage and the 19th Amendment to the Constitution, giving women the right to vote for the first time in American history. By March, thirty-five States had ratified it, and it needed only one more to make it the law of the land. It was pretty much a foregone conclusion that, come November, women would be allowed to cast their ballots in the presidential election. Sure enough, on August

18, Tennessee became number 36. How that might affect the outcome of the election was a frequent topic of discussion around the dairy and at home.

When the subject came up one evening at dinner with Eugene visiting, he opined, "My daddy says it won't matter much in Florida. Most wives, if they'll vote at all, will vote like their husbands." Then he looked at Janie and said, "You will do that for me, too, won't you, sweetheart?"

Janie blushed and said amiably, "Of course, I will, but I don't think much about politics."

Eugene smiled smugly and continued, oblivious to Essie's presence in the kitchen, "My dad says the issue is how the niggers and their women will vote. A lot of them are troublemakers and will cast their ballots for the Republicans."

Grandpa nodded in agreement, but Papa took a second helping of beans, appearing uninterested in the conversation. Lizzie and I looked at each other and shrugged. We didn't understand what all the fuss was about, and we really didn't care. But then I noticed Essie listening from behind the doorway. Her lips were tight and eyes were flashing with anger.

When dinner was over, Eugene and Janie went off to a dance in Winter Garden, and Papa and Grandpa smoked their nightly cigars in the living room. Lizzie withdrew to the bedroom to do homework and I sought out Essie in the kitchen to find out why she was so upset.

She was doing the dishes and acted as if nothing had happened, but I asked, "Why is voting so important?"

Essie looked at me, deliberating. Then she handed me a towel to help with drying, and we worked side by side in silence for a while. Slowly, she started to speak in a low, murmuring voice. "It matters, Georgia, it matters a lot, to us and to you, as well. For too many years we've been treated like second class citizens. The Declaration of Independence says 'All men are created equal,' but it left out more than half the people in this country. Now it's finally our turn, and that young whipper-snapper thinks we're just going to do what our men folk tell us to do."

I knew Essie had gone to meetings in the Methodist Quarters north of Tullulah and listened to speakers who came from out of town, and she sounded like she was repeating stuff they might have said. But the passion in her voice was unmistakable.

"My mother was a slave and I was born free, but I don't have the same rights as Jim, and he doesn't have the same rights as that white boy who talks like the cock of the walk. It's got to change. I want Little Jim to grow up equal and proud, without Jim Crow."

"So you're going to vote?"

"I am," she said, adding with defiance in her voice, "and I'm gonna' make up my own mind. And according to the Black Dispatch, the other Negro women are too!"

Florida didn't vote on the Nineteenth Amendment at all as three more States ratified it over the next couple of years. It wasn't until May 13, 1969, that the Sunshine State finally got on the right side of history with women suffrage, although it wasn't the last. Five southern states—South and North Carolina, Georgia, Mississippi and Louisiana—passed the amendment even later.

Essie was not alone among black housekeepers in her championing of voting. For years, black women all over the south had encouraged their men to vote, believing that the ballot box would provide them with a path to the freedom and equality they all sought. Ever since the dismantling of Reconstruction and the institutionalization of

Jim Crow, the Democratic Party had a stranglehold on state legislatures and governorships in the South. Black leaders understood that the only way they could achieve their goals was to get rid of one party rule in Florida.

As early as January 1, 1919—commemorating the day the Emancipation Proclamation went into effect during the Civil War—African Americans in Jacksonville, Florida, had called for the start of a voter registration movement. Within several months, black voter registration campaigns started up in 28 counties and spread throughout the state in order to break the hold of white supremacy. All over Florida, meetings were held in churches and people's homes to discuss how to make a difference in the presidential elections by voting Republican the following year.

One of the main stumbling blocks encountered in their desire to reclaim the "Party of Lincoln" was the poll tax that every citizen who wished to vote had to pay when registering. Florida required paying double the amount of the poll tax, two years' worth, making it especially difficult for poor African Americans. Not until 1964, when the Twenty-fourth Amendment of the U.S. Constitution was ratified, did poll taxes become illegal throughout the nation.

In the meantime, black men and women strategized on how to deal with the problem. They organized drives to raise money to pay the poll tax for those who could not afford it themselves.

The passage of the 19th Amendment gave voice to another sizable, disenfranchised, black population. As first time voters, women were exempt from the poll tax and, with an organizational network in place throughout Florida, they registered in droves. In many communities, they outnumbered white women voters who didn't register with the same passion, threatening to alter the decade's long control of the Democrat party and striking fear into the hearts of white supremacists.

With blacks beginning to flex their political muscles, younger African Americans became more confident, and relations between the races became more contentious. As the national elections neared, every strained encounter of blacks and whites threatened to ignite and fan the flames of an increasingly tense situation.

MOUNTING TENSIONS

One Saturday night in early September many of the residents of Ocoee went by section-gang lever car to an area dance in Clarcona. Janie and Eugene were very excited, having done it before when the Pike family car was unavailable. I was a bit surprised that my sister enjoyed helping operate the hand crank on the railcar and travel in the open air on the tracks for the three-mile journey.

"It's fun!" she said enthusiastically.

The dance was one of the big social events of the early fall and most of the white men in Ocoee and their wives went and had a good time. But when they got back, many received shocking news.

While they were gone, a group of Negroes went from one white residence to another, apparently trying to put a scare into the remaining residents. The next day, Ned came over to our house, bubbling over with all kinds of news and information. He told Lizzie and me that he heard they stopped at the house of J.R. Pounds ready to cause trouble. They didn't count on Mr. Pound's son-in-law, Sam Salisbury, being home, who got his pistol and confronted them at a side door.

"He waved his pistol right in their faces," Ned said, excitement glittering in his eyes.

Ned loved rumors and liked to exaggerate. It was known that Colonel Salisbury, as he was known in Ocoee, had been to West Point, and had been police chief in Orlando, so I could imagine him standing his ground. It helped that Mr. Pounds was well liked by many of the blacks in the community, and after some discussion the blacks went away. But they went to other houses all over town after and, although they committed no acts of violence, they scared a lot of the white folks.

That Sunday evening, Eugene came over to dinner, outraged at what had happened. "Something has to be done," he sputtered.

Papa calmed him down saying, "It's just youngsters getting a bit out of hand. No reason to get overexcited. Let cooler heads prevail."

Eugene did calm down, but I could see he was churning inside.

I wanted to talk to Essie about what had happened, but all she said was, "Those boys didn't act right, and they'll get a talking to." Then she went on washing dishes and I could tell the subject was closed.

Papa was right, though. Two days later, three prominent white city fathers met with July Perry and the minister of the black church and had a discussion about it, and that was the end of it. No further incidents of that nature occurred.

A more serious matter took place a few days later, when a young Negro, Ronnie Petsey, forced an older white man, Peach Griffin, off the road coming from Spring Lake to Ocoee. When he did it again to another man in town, a group of white men went after him and shot him in the leg. Worse would have happened to him, for sure, but even though he was wounded, he ran like the wind to safety at July

Perry's house, who was his uncle. Although the incident was reported to the sheriff, no one was ever arrested for the shooting.

Everyone who came to the dairy to buy milk had an opinion about it, but only our white customers had their say. Most of them thought Ronnie Petsey got off lightly. A few insisted that he should have been lynched. I was shocked when I heard that. They didn't say it in the presence of any of our Negro customers, but I could tell they really meant it.

They also complained that it was getting harder and harder for them to get into the three grocery stores in downtown Ocoee to shop because groups of blacks would gather at the front doors, milling around and socializing.

"They're loud and noisy and don't step aside. It feels like being run through a gauntlet," said Mr. Jackson, an older white man.

Grandpa agreed with the milder griping, although he never condoned the calls for violence. But Papa never let on how he felt about what his customers were saying. He'd nod and clear his throat, but never argued or contributed to the conversation. He made sure he got along well with everybody.

One time, after a particularly angry white customer left the store, he sighed, turned to Grandpa and said, "I understand how the store owners feel. I'm sure they're not happy, but they're reluctant to tell the Negroes to go away because most of their trade with them is based on credit, and they're afraid the Negroes will get mad and not pay their bills."

Grandpa agreed, "They'd be left high and dry with no money and have a hard time trying to stay open."

There was also a lot of talk about the upcoming election. Some customers mentioned that the Klan was warning "niggers" not to vote. One man started to rant about Judge Cheney, a Ree-publican in Orlando, coming to talk to local Negroes about defying the Klan.

When I asked Essie about him she said that there had been gossip on the Black Dispatch—the informal grapevine by which the local Negroes spread news among themselves faster than anyone else in the area– that he'd been meeting with July Perry and Mose Norman about registering all eligible black men and women to vote who were in District#10. Our district runs from Windermere-Crown Point Road on the west, Fullers Cross Road-Apopka Clarcona Road on the north, Apopka-Vineland Road on the east, and Moore-Gotha Roads on the south. We are a very big district.

She lowered her voice and said, "At first we were suspicious of him, but then it turned out that he is a Free Mason. Many of the leaders in the black community are Free Masons, too, and therefore brothers. And brothers take care of one another."

Late in September Essie and Big Jim asked to be off for a whole weekend, except for the cow milking at the dairy, of course, because some of the men in the Northern Quarters were having a "raising bee" for Jesse Surrencey and his family, or as some called it a "barn raising." Winter was coming and the Surrenceys could not afford to build a barn unless the whole community came together to help. Big Jim said the barn would be ready for paint on Monday, if everybody showed up, and hay could be brought in on Tuesday. It seemed fast to me but I was glad Essie and Big Jim would be back at our house on Monday.

Big Jim was excited because he would be one of the lead carpenters along with Mose Norman. He laughed and said, "Mose will surely be late so he can show off his shiny car as he drives around the quarters. I hope he knows how to work because we have to join and dowel the beams to make the barn steady in the wind."

Little Jim was excited, too, because he and some of the other older boys would be fetching tools and parts. The younger children would watch and help the women too, as they provide water, lemonade and food for the men.

That Saturday, we all got up early to pitch in, even Janie. Lizzie and I were surprised because she usually had her head in the clouds and no time for anyone but her wonderful Eugene. Only Big Jim showed up, saying that Essie and the other women in the Northern Quarters were getting food ready for the day. He worked with the energy of two men instead, and we were done with the milking at the regular time.

Papa told him, "Help me load up the truck for deliveries and I'll drive you to the Surrenceys. It'll save you at least half an hour."

Big Jim thanked him, and when the time came I asked to go along. I'd never been to a raising bee and wanted to see for myself. Papa agreed—I could help him make deliveries—and we drove off.

As we drove around Starke Lake—with me scrunched between Papa and Big Jim—the weather was picture perfect, not a cloud in the sky, and one of the first fall days when it wasn't so humid. North of Tullulah, we took a turn onto a dirt road and soon came to a meadow and a clapboard house. There was a car parked, a sedan with the top down, and we pulled up behind it.

Further on, I saw a truck that looked like July Perry's, loaded with yellow pine boards, standing near the beginnings of the barn. Some men were putting up big vertical timbers at the corners, steadying and holding them in place with ropes, waiting for the crossbeams. Others were working on constructing the skeleton for the front wall that had been laid out on the ground. I could hear the sharp rasping of saws and the hammers striking nails and dowels.

Off to one side near their homestead, Essie and other women were putting up tables and preparing food and drink. Little Jim looked up from a plank he was trying to lay across two saw horses. He recognized our truck and waved to us.

As Big Jim got out, Papa handed him a big hunk of cheese wrapped in paper and said, "Take two of the bottles of chocolate milk, too. The kids will like it."

Big Jim said, "Thank you Mr. Kambel, but you don't have to do that."

Papa waved him off and Big Jim went to the back of the truck and pulled out the milk.

I recognized July Perry, standing by the wall, looking like he was in charge. He wore his wide-brimmed hat, but had put his coat aside. He looked over toward us and nodded in greeting in our direction.

Meanwhile, Mose Norman came up on Papa's side of the truck, wiped the sweat from his forehead and said, "Hello, Mr. Kambel. Hello, Miss Georgia. Glad you came and brought Big Jim. We can sure use him and I can use a break."

Papa nodded and gazed at the beginnings of the barn. "I can see that, Mose. You've got your work cut out for you."

I was surprised to see Mose in rough work pants and an undershirt. He was normally dressed to the nines, wearing a dark coat and tie and a fancy hat. He wiped the sweat from his forehead and said, "We've been hard at work since sun up."

Pointing to the shiny black roadster parked in front of us, Papa asked, "Is that a new car?"

A smile blossomed on Mose's face, a mixture of deep pleasure and pride. "Yup. Drives like the wind."

Just then, someone called out, "Mose, we need you."

"Good talking to you," said Papa.

With just a touch of regret, Mose left and joined the rest of the men who were lining up by the wall they'd built.

We stayed in the truck and watched as July Perry called out, "One, two, three, heave!" The men with the ropes put their back into it, and pulled with all their strength, their arm and shoulder muscles straining and bulging. All the women and kids stopped what they were doing and watched, too. July kept calling out the cadence and slowly, haltingly, the skeleton wall started to rise until it was upright, swaying a bit in the morning breeze. Everyone cheered and Little Jim with some of the other kids jumped up and down in excitement. Quickly the men lashed the wall to the upright beams and started drilling holes and driving dowels through to make it fast. I heard Big Jim yelling out from time to time, telling someone what to do and calling for more dowels.

Papa glanced at me and said, "I know you'd like to stay and watch some more, but we have to get going."

I waved to Essie and Little Jim as Papa backed up the truck to a spot where he could turn around. I felt excited and could imagine how good it must feel to come together and build something big and useful. "So what happens next?" I asked.

Papa put the truck into forward gear and, as we made our way down the side roads, said, "They'll do the other walls the same way, then add rafters and the roof, and put on the side boards. Then Jesse will climb on the roof and put a flag at the top of the gables. It's called a topping out for good luck. Everyone will raise a cup of white lighting in a toast and then they'll eat and the fiddle music starts for the barn dancing."

I couldn't wait until Monday to see Little Jim and hear all about it from him.

ELECTION EVE

That was the last time I can remember people coming together as a community. With the approaching election, things became more and more strained both in town and around the dinner table, especially when Eugene came over. He loved Essie's cooking, in particular her fried chicken and little biscuits, and said so on several occasions, although he never gave her credit or thanked her the way Papa and Grandpa did.

The week before the elections, he shot his mouth off about the Negro threat to white supremacy. Apparently, more black than white women had registered to vote in Orange County, surprising and worrying the Democrats, most of whom were in the Klan. But he had his harshest words for Judge Cheney, who had owned the Orlando Light and Power Company, and was running for the U.S. Senate as a Republican. He and William O'Neal, another civic leader, went to black church meetings to talk about voter registration and were meeting "in secret" with July Perry and Mose Norman, as if anything like that could be kept quiet in Ocoee.

"They're traitors to our race, advising the niggers in this town on how to vote," he fumed. But we'll see about that! We'll make sure none of them make it to the ballot box!"

My dad says it's time someone teaches July Perry and Mose Norman a lesson!"

He went on until Papa finally said, "I think we'll table all discussion about politics for now."

Eugene flushed red, being called on the carpet like that, but he acquiesced. I glanced at Janie. I could tell she was embarrassed for him. She said nothing but put her hand on his and squeezed it, as if she was agreeing with him.

Papa changed the subject.

That morning at the dairy, Justice of the Peace, R.C. Bigelow, had come in and asked if we had a notion of the best place where to catch some fish. Surprised, Papa told him, "Bigelow, you're from Ocoee and you know where we usually go for good fishing. In fact, I know you're favorite fishing spot is right here at Starke Lake." At that point, the justice said that he wanted to go further afield for a get-away trip, and Papa suggested Lake Monroe in Sanford as a good place with a good days catch. Still, he thought it an odd request.

Eugene smirked loudly and said, "Sanford should be far enough away!"

Papa looked at him strangely and was about to ask what he meant when Grandpa proudly announced that he was going to a Civil War Convention over the weekend right here in Orlando. We all knew he had traveled far and wide to many conventions because he took every opportunity to wear his medals and Confederate uniform, and he wasn't about to miss a get-together happening right in his backyard. He looked at me and said, "You'll have to polish my medals again and get them good and shiny. They've tarnished a little since the last time I wore them."

Eugene said, "Boy I'd like to be at that convention."

After dinner, when I helped to clear the table and went into the kitchen, Essie was clearing away leftovers. I never saw her so furious. Her normally kind features were hardened into a mean-looking mask. Her lips were puckered into an angry sneer. When I started to ask her a question, she held up her hand, silencing me. I knew better than to pursue it and went about my business quietly. It was obvious that Eugene shooting his mouth off at dinner is what had enraged her.

Friday came and Grandpa was ready to go to his Convention, handsomely dressed in his gray uniform, with his Confederate medals shining in the sunlight. Papa put his bag in the truck and the two of them headed for Orlando where Grandpa would spend the night. It was quiet and lonesome without him around the house.

Saturday afternoon Papa asked Lizzie and me if we wanted to ride with him to pick up Grandpa. He said, "There will be a big crowd because vets from WW I, the Daughters of the American Revolution, and the Boy Scouts are all at the event this year."

Of course, we said yes. There was nothing going on in Ocoee. It took us less time to drive to downtown Orlando than to find Grandpa in the crowd, but we finally spotted him talking to other men his age in uniform. None of them had as many medals pinned on their chest as him. Papa carried his bag to where we'd parked the truck and threw it in the back. Grandpa got in the front while we climbed in the back and settled in. We weren't worried about getting jostled. We'd never had any trouble holding on because Papa always drove more slowly than normal when we rode in the back.

As we got to the corner where we'd have to turn to head out of town, there was a street barricade that stopped us. Lizzie and I stood up and leaned over the cabin to get a good view of what was going on. I wish I hadn't. I've never seen such a scary sight!

It was a Ku Klux Klan parade. First came three figures on horseback, wearing white robes and pointed white cowls. They were followed by rows upon rows of Klansmen marching in step. Their white robes reached more than halfway down their calves to where their black pants and shoes were visible. Some of them carried American flags. It was an eerie, terrifying sight in the dimming light of dusk, reinforced by their menacing silence. Only their footsteps on the pavement could be heard, a ghostly army bent on intimidation and unspoken threats. The spectators, many from the convention, watched. The only words spoken were when one of the horsemen yelled from time to time, "We are marching a million strong throughout the South tonight."

It took a long time for all the robed men to pass. As the police removed the barricades, Papa got out and had us climb into the front of the truck. He had a stern look on his face as he maneuvered through the remaining crowd, milling about after the parade. When we got clear, he sped up and drove home as fast as the road would allow. We sat scrunched between him and Grandpa in silence. We knew not to say a word.

When we got to our homestead, Eugene and Janie were sitting on a bench on the front porch, holding hands. While Grandpa changed out of his uniform and we got ready for supper, we shared what we had seen.

Eugene straightened up and told us with glowing eyes that a smaller number of KKK members had marched in Winter Garden earlier that night. He had seen it himself and it had made him proud. I was glad that he kept the rest of what he was thinking to himself.

Later that night I was thankful to finally be back to the homestead, safely tucked into my bed, but I couldn't get the KKK marchers out of my head! They were much more ominous and more frightening than when Ned, Lizzie and I found that KKK suit or the time we flummoxed the Klan rally at the lake.

By the time I was up on Sunday, Papa had already gone out and gotten a copy of the *Orlando Morning Sentinel*, which was unusual. Bold headlines on the front page of the newspaper announced:

Clansmen Cowled in Flowing White, Parade in Orlando's Streets More than Five Hundred Strong

When Papa read from the article that "a veil of mystery hangs over the movement of the 'white cavalcade,' a mystery that no one on the streets dared to lift, only to remind all that the Old South still lives," It sent cold chills all over my body. I had a pretty good idea what that mystery was all about, and so did everybody else.

Essie and Big Jim came to the homestead after church to tidy up and to start supper. They were heading inside when Big Jim told Papa and Grandpa that everyone in the Northern Quarters knew about the march in Orlando, and the KKK trying to scare off black voters, but it would make no difference.

July Perry had seen the Sunday morning paper and told everyone at church that it wasn't anything new. He said, "I know the power of the Klan for sure. But, what is first on my mind is that, come Tuesday, I am going to vote in the Presidential Election and cast my ballot for Warren G. Harding!" He added, "I have been assured that as long as I registered and paid my poll tax, I can vote as Mose Norman and I did in the Presidential Election of 1916, and so can you!"

Later on Essie told me, "Me and all of my friends in the Northern Quarters have registered. We are all going to vote come Tuesday. If we want to be first class citizens, it is high time we get out there and vote."

ॐ

No doubt, the KKK made a strong impression on Central Florida that Saturday night of October 30, 1920. These marches, and there were more in other communities as well, including in Daytona and Jacksonville, were warnings to all African Americans and their sympathizers to stay home on election day.

In the case of Judge Cheney and William O'Neal, secretary of the Republican campaign committee, the KKK went even farther. The Grandmaster of the Florida Ku Klux Klan sent them a threatening letter, chastising them for going out among the Negroes of Orange County and delivering lectures, explaining to them just how to become citizens and how to assert their rights. Then he warned,

> *If you are familiar with the history of the days of reconstruction which flowed in the wake of the Civil War, you will recall that the "Scallawags" of the north, and the Republicans of the south proceeded very much the same. You are proceeding, to instill in the negro the idea of social equality. You will also remember that these things forced the loyal citizens of the south to organize clans of determined men, who pledged themselves to maintain white supremacy and to safeguard our women and children.*
>
> *And now if you are a scholar you know that history repeats itself and he who resorts to your kind of game is handing edged tools. We have always enjoyed WHITE SUPREMACY in this country and he who interferes must face the consequences.*

The Klan and the Democrats and white supremacists had reasons to be worried. Their concerted efforts to discourage, intimidate and prevent blacks from registering to vote had been unsuccessful. In Orange County—Orlando and surrounding communities—the week after the passage of the amendment granting women the right to vote, 369 registered. Only three percent were men, the rest were women. African-American women made up the rolls by a margin of fifteen to one!

No wonder the Klan got involved and began warning the black community in Ocoee that "not a single Negro would be permitted to vote."

But their warnings were no longer heeded. Black communities were heartened by their successful organizing of voter drives utilizing the Knights of Pythias, an African-American fraternal order, churches, and women's groups. They believed the tide was turning in their favor. In addition, there were black Masons who established close ties with their white counterparts in anticipation of the election. In Orlando and Ocoee, for example, Judge Cheney, July Perry and Mose Norman were all Masons and may have developed a sense of trust, despite the fact that the white Masonic order also contained a large number of KKK members.

In any case, battle lines were drawn, and African Americans all over Florida were poised to make their vote count.

13

ELECTION DAY

Papa woke us earlier than usual on that Tuesday morning in November and told us to get breakfast ready quickly because we had to go to the dairy as soon as possible. When I asked where Essie was, he said, "She and Big Jim aren't coming in today. They have some chores to take care of at their house."

It was an odd thing to say, as if he didn't think we knew what was going on. It was Election Day and they were getting ready to vote. Of course, we knew. Our teacher had told us that school was canceled, which was a big deal. Papa also wasn't aware of how much I had talked to Essie about the elections and all she had shared with me.

We had a cold breakfast of bread, butter, cheese and jam with none of the usual conversation. Then we drove to the dairy. Even Janie, who usually had her head in the clouds, thinking about her wonderful Eugene, came along to help with washing bottles, milking the cows, and getting the truck ready for deliveries. Sarah was there already and, to my surprise Ned showed up to help out, too. David was conspicuously absent. At some point, Sarah mentioned that she hadn't seen any of the blacks who worked at the dairy. Ned, who seemed nervous or excited or something, said, "There is going to be trouble at the polls when the niggers show up to vote. The KKK has warned them all not to go, or else."

It put me on edge, worrying about Essie and her family.

Without our best worker, Papa had difficulty managing herding the cows into the barn, and it took us twice as long as normal to get all the milking done. The last heifers in the queue were lowing in discomfort from having to wait so long with their udders heavy and full. I thought it was odd that Papa and Grandpa didn't ask Sarah where David was because it put a hardship on the entire dairy.

I wondered what he was up to and I bet Eugene wasn't far behind. I didn't know if they belonged to the Klan, although I was pretty sure Eugene's dad did.

When Papa had finished loading the Oakland dairy order onto the truck, Grandpa said, "I might as well ride shot gun and see what is going on with this Election Day." We all knew what he meant!

I spoke up. "I want to come, too. You'll need help carrying all the bottles."

Papa and Grandpa exchanged a look, and Papa said, "I guess it'll be all right."

It was a gray day and the roads were eerily quiet. The clouds seemed to get heavier as the morning progressed, but it didn't rain.

When we approached Oak Hill, the Carrington Estate, to deliver their order, I noticed there were no black men working the grounds, not even down by the lake. Papa and I got out of the truck and I carried the milk bottles, feeling important. He was about to knock on the side door to the kitchen when it opened. To our surprise, it was not Lena, the black maid, but Mrs. Carrington who opened the door. She must have seen us pull up and said, "Come on in. You can put the bottles on the kitchen table, Georgia."

Papa shot me a warning glance when I asked, "Did all the help decide to take the day off?"

But Mrs. Carrington didn't seem to mind. She said, "Since it is Election Day, my husband thought it would be best for the help to be at their own homes and not out on the roads traveling."

Papa nodded in understanding, but I felt the awkwardness and tension in the air.

As Mrs. Carrington ushered us out, she told us, "Thank you for coming over today and please tell Grandpa Kambel hello."

We said we would and continued on our way. After we finished all the deliveries, we headed back to the dairy.

As we were about to turn into our drive we saw Mr. Bigelow, the Justice of the Peace and election official, heading out of town. He pulled his car over and Papa did the same with the truck. Bigelow looked serious but relieved somehow. Leaning out of his window, he called out, "Just want to let you know that a couple of blacks have voted, so you might want to get down there and cast your vote soon."

Then he drove off, trailing a cloud of dust behind him.

Papa got out at the dairy to see if everything was okay. Ned had left and Sarah was putting out eggs that her parents had brought in from their chicken coop.

Janie asked, seemingly bored, "Can I go home now?"

I looked at her, a bit exasperated. "Aren't you going to vote?"

Shrugging, Janie said, "Eugene said he'd pick me up later and take me."

Smiling kindly, Papa said, "All right, but we'll need you this afternoon again." Then he looked at Lizzie and me. "You girls stay and help Sarah while Grandpa and I go to the polls to vote."

I piped up again, "I want to come with you." Papa was about to say no, so I quickly said, "I'm not a little girl."

To my surprise, Sarah said, "Oh, go on, Mr. Kambel. It will be a slow day here, and she'll just drive us nuts."

Papa couldn't help but smile at that. "All right. But you stay in the truck the whole time, no matter what happens."

I nodded vigorously and climbed up into the truck. I was excited, but also on edge, squeezed between Papa and Grandpa, as we headed to downtown Ocoee. Along the way, Papa explained that the Ocoee District #10 included Clarcona and Gotha, two smaller nearby communities.

We got there shortly before noon and Papa found a parking spot by the dry goods store across the street from the tan colored building where the polls were. There was a crowd of mostly men milling around outside, gossiping. I didn't see any black faces anywhere, but I was surprised to see David among them. Papa and Grandpa got out and said hello to a couple of Woodmen of the World friends of theirs and other people they knew, and everything seemed hunky dory.

They went inside and I wish I could have gone with them to see what they had to do and what casting their vote meant. I planned to ask them about it when they came back.

Suddenly, a shiny new car drove up and parked in front of our truck. Inside were Mose Norman and July Perry. They got out, dressed like they were going to church. As they headed across the street all conversations stopped and everyone in the crowd watched warily as they took off their hats and went into the polling station.

Soon we heard shouting coming from inside like there was an altercation, and Mose and July stormed out, looking furious. At the door, Mose turned and yelled, "I paid my poll tax and we'll be back!" Then they got into the car, slammed the doors, and drove off.

Soon Papa and Grandpa came out, looking grim-faced. They stopped and talked to some of their friends for a spell, then came over and got into the truck. I was on pins and nee-dles to find out what had happened and blurted out, "What's going on?"

Papa started the truck and pulled into the street. As we headed back to the dairy, he finally explained, "When Mose and July came in to vote, the poll workers told them that they couldn't because there were no records that they had regis-tered or paid the poll tax. Mose and July argued, but the poll workers wouldn't budge and turned them away."

Grandpa added, "That Mose has a mouth on him that'll get him into trouble in no time!"

"What are they going to do?" I asked, worried about what might happen to Essie and Big Jim when they tried to vote.

"I heard July tell Mose to drive to Orlando so they could talk to Judge Cheney," Papa said. "I hope he talks some sense into them and they don't stir up any more trouble."

What happened in Ocoee was a microcosm of things taking place all over Florida. Officials threatened to arrest black voters. While black men and women managed to cast their ballots in a few towns by showing up in force—Gifford, Daytona, St. Augustine—in most com-munities, white intimidation practices won out. Carloads of heavily armed white men patrolled the access to polling places. Armed white deputies stood guard at the entrances to voting precinct buildings, looking menacing and, in some cases, threatening to arrest any blacks trying to vote.

With fear of a Republican victory, Democrats in Winter Garden tacked a black flag on a big oak tree near the polls with a picture of Warren G. Harding surrounded by Negro candidates from other states. The white men milling about kept shouting, "We'd rather be dead than live under Black Republicanism."

Many places had separate lines for black and white voters. The queues for whites moved quickly and the lines for blacks were slow as molasses. Some prospective black voters stood in the hot sun for hours, waiting for their turn. In Miami, blacks were not allowed to vote until all whites had cast their votes. Towards closing time many who had waited patiently were driven away by a white crowd. Even voters, who brought with them certificates saying they had registered, were told that their names were not in the registration books.

ESCALATION

A round four in the afternoon, we were getting ready for the second milking of the day when Jason Farmer, one of Papa's Woodmen of the World friends, came by. He took Papa and Grandpa outside out of earshot, but we sneaked up to a window that was ajar and listened to their conversation anyway.

Mr. Farmer had been inside at the polling station when Mose Norman came back in his car. He was like a man on a mission. Apparently, he and July Perry had seen Judge Cheney in Orlando and told him what had happened to them at the Ocoee polls. The Judge insisted that, of course, they could vote and gave them a note from him saying so. He had also told them to get their certificates of registration and poll tax receipts and to write down the name of the poll workers who were keeping them from voting. Brandishing pieces of paper, Mose was threatening to do that. He shouted that he'd voted in the 1916 election, and he wasn't going to let anyone deprive him of his rights this time around!

Kent Culpepper told Mose that any voting irregularity had to be taken up with Mr. Bigelow, the Justice of the Peace, except he'd gone for the day and wouldn't be back 'till the following day. Kent smirked when he said it, knowing full well that Bigelow had made sure to be out of town on purpose, which got Mose even more upset.

While that commotion was going on inside the polling station, some of the people on the street went to Mose's car and saw a shotgun in the back seat. One of the men checked it out and said, "It is loaded!" That got everyone upset and righteously angry and some of the crowd went inside the building looking for Mose.

Mr. Douglas' daughters, Rachel and Regina, were in the dry goods store across the street, on the second floor picking out material for dresses, and they saw and heard the whole thing through the open window. The white men emerged, pushing and shoving Mose so that he stumbled and almost fell. One of them whacked him in the head with the handle of his own shotgun. Regina nearly fainted when she saw the blood pouring from his forehead. Mose managed to fight them off long enough to jump into his car and take off for the Northern Quarters. A few of the men ran after him but soon gave up.

Grandpa harrumphed. "I knew that boy's temper would get him into trouble. I just hope it doesn't get him killed."

After Mr. Farmer left, Papa came inside. He looked more serious than I had ever seen him before. He ran his fingers through his hair like someone who'd gotten terrible news and didn't know what to do. He sat down heavily on one of the stools behind the counter and we crowded around him and peppered him with questions that told him we already knew most of it. "Is Mose going to be all right?" "What's going to happen?"

Grandpa joined in, shaking his head, "This doesn't look good. There's sure to be more trouble."

Papa looked at our worried expressions, got up and said, "We better get the cows milked."

By then Janie had joined us and we all started herding the big Guernsey heifers into the barn. We worked in dead silence. The cows must have sensed how tense we were because they kept moving around and didn't want to settle down. We had to whack them on their sides to get them to stand still.

I tried to concentrate on the task, but my mind kept wandering. It sounded odd when Grandpa had called Mose Norman "that boy." Mose was at least 55 years old and Grandpa never called Big Jim that, who was a good ten years younger.

At some point, Janie asked, disappointed, "Isn't anybody going to ask me about who I voted for?"

She liked to be the center of attention and obviously hadn't heard about the scuffle, which must have occurred after she had been there.

Papa indulged her. "Well?"

"I cast my vote for James A. Cox for president and Duncan U. Fletcher for the U.S. Senate," she said proudly.

It only made sense that she'd voted for the Democrat candidates, no doubt on Eugene's advice, since she knew nothing about politics.

Around the time we finished with the milking, David and Eugene came by the dairy to see Janie and Sarah. They both had severe expressions on their faces, yet seemed oddly wound up. Eugene blurted out that Burley Jones, an older black man who was an ex-slave and lived in the Southern Quarters, had come around to warn that "the niggers were accumulating down at July Perry's house planning to cause trouble."

David drew himself up to his full height and said, "We're on our way to make sure that doesn't happen."

Sarah fretted, "What are you going to do?"

"Colonel Salisbury is getting a posse together to arrest July Perry, and we're going to go with him," David answered manfully.

Janie's hand flew to her mouth and Eugene took her hand and said, "Now don't you worry. We'll have a lot of men and nothing serious is going to happen. I'll see you later tonight."

But after they left, Janie kept wringing her hands. Sarah was anxious, too, and Papa said, "We can close up here ourselves. You run along home, now."

Sarah gave him a grateful smile and took off.

It was dusk by the time we got back to our homestead. We should have been tired from the long day, but we were all wound up from the worrying and having to bide our time, not knowing what was going on and fearing the worst. I knew things were very serious when Papa and Grandpa brought out their shotgun and hunting rifles, loaded them, and put them on the table next to the front door.

Meanwhile, Lizzie and I laid out a cold collation for supper in the dining room. But when we sat down, we weren't all that hungry. Janie kept poking at her food, worried about Eugene.

Very soon we heard gun shots coming from the Northern Quarters. There were so many it sounded like fire crackers on the Fourth of July, but we knew what they were. Old Blue was so scared he started to yelp and run around like crazy. We all rushed out back and looked across Starke Lake, but we couldn't see anything. We went back inside and hunkered down, worried about what was happening.

It was dark when we heard a call from the front of the house. We all went on the front porch and saw Ned. He was out of breath and his face was smudged with dirt. His eyes were wide with shock and the words tumbled from his mouth like a waterfall. When he calmed down a bit, he told us that he'd followed the posse marching up the Ocoee-Apopka Road to the Northern Quarters. Led by Colonel Salisbury, they all carried rifles and shotguns. When they got to July Perry's house, Ned hid behind the trees lining the front yard on one side and watched. Some of the men sneaked around to the backyard to surround the house.

At some point the Colonel went up on the front porch and knocked on the door. He called out, "July, we want to talk to you. Come out!"

When July opened the door, carrying a lantern, the Colonel said, "You need to come with us."

July said, "Yas, Suh, boss. Let me git my coat."

As he turned, the Colonel grabbed him. In the struggle, he pounded July on the head with the butt of his rifle.

Suddenly a shot rang out from inside the house. The Colonel cried out and fell to the ground. He was holding his arm like he'd been hit there and rolled off the porch to safety.

Then things went haywire and all hell broke loose. Everybody started shooting at once and there were screams from inside the house and the backyard. The gun battle went on for a long time, followed by an eerie silence. People everywhere looked dazed and confused until there was shouting from the side yard, "Help! We've got two bodies over here, two of ours!"

All at once, everybody was yelling.

Ned said, "I was so scared, my heart almost stopped."

Janie cried out "What about Eugene? Is he okay?"

Ned looked uncertain. "I don't know. I just know everyone pulled back, and I took off running and came here."

Papa put his arms around Janie and said, "Thank you for telling us, Ned. You go home now to your mama and papa. They must be worried sick."

For a moment, Ned looked like a lost boy. Then he wrinkled his nose and nodded. His head kept bobbing up and down as he walked into the darkness. We were all shaken and Papa told us to put Old Blue inside tonight.

Ned wasn't gone for long before a car came to a screeching halt in front of our house. There were two men sitting in the front. Papa went outside to find out what they wanted. We watched anxiously through the porch windows. They talked for some time, and then the car swung around and drove away.

When Papa got back in the house, he was white as a ghost. In a halting voice, he told us that several of the men in the posse had been wounded in the gun battle, including Colonel Salisbury, and that two white men had been killed, Elmer McDaniel of Ocoee and Leo Borgard of Winter Garden. The survivors put the two bodies on a wagon to take them to their families. There was no sign of July Perry, his family, or the other men in his house. They had escaped in the confusion after the battle.

Papa looked at Janie. "I guess Eugene is all right."

She burst into tears and ran from the room. Papa gestured to Lizzie and she went after her. Then he continued, "The news of the gun battle is spreading like wild fire. They've called for Orange County sheriff Frank Gordon and reinforcements from Orlando."

Grandpa said, "Borgard and McDaniel were Klansmen. The KKK from Winter Garden and Apopka will be out in force in no time, looking for revenge. They'll surely–"

Papa shot him a warning glance and he stopped in mid-sentence. I was mortified, and it must have shown on my face because Grandpa looked stricken and apologetic.

Lizzie and Janie came back into the living room and we all sat down together. We were too wound up to go to sleep, but we didn't have anything to say either. So we kept each other company, trapped inside our own thoughts, waiting, knowing the evening wasn't over. I was bewildered. I kept trying to understand why everyone had gotten so riled up about Mose and other blacks wanting to vote.

Soon we heard cars and trucks drive down the road outside toward Ocoee and the Northern Quarters. Sometime later there were volleys of gunshots, not as intense as before, but echoing across the lake just the same. When we went to the window, we saw flames start to flicker above the trees and, before long, they grew bigger and wider and lit up the sky. From time to time, we could hear the popping of explosions, like logs in a fireplace, only ten times as loud. We watched in shock. The whole Northern Quarters was ablaze!

I was so scared for Essie, Big Jim and Little Jim.

I don't remember how much time passed, but at some point, Old Blue started yelping and running through the house, signaling there was something or someone out on the porch. Papa and Grandpa went to the front door and grabbed their hunting rifles while the rest of us crouched anxiously at the entrance to the living room.

When Papa called out, "Who is it?" A muffled voice answered from the porch, "Mr. Ed, it's me—Essie—and Little Jim."

Papa took the lantern off the side table and opening the door, thrust it into the darkness outside. We all crowded behind him trying to see. In the flickering light, we could make out Essie looking terrified. Her paisley dress was torn in a few places and her hair disheveled. Little Jim was standing next to her with eyes big as saucers, holding his new puppy in his trembling arms.

Papa asked, "Where is Big Jim?"

An anguished cry escaped Essie's lips. "I don't know, Mr. Ed, I don't know. He went off to help our neighbors. He told me to come here with Little Jim, and I'm worried sick about him." She started to moan and sway back and forth. "I don't know what to do! I don't know what to do!"

I had never seen her so distraught and flustered, and it upset me terribly.

Papa said, "Come inside," and started to put his arm around her.

She clutched his hand so hard that her knuckles turned white and pleaded, "Can you go looking for him?"

Gently removing unclasping her fingers, Papa said, "Big Jim is smart. He's probably hiding some place where nobody can find him. He'll be all right. Come on in."

Essie nodded desperately but let him walk her into the house. Little Jim trailed behind her. Lizzie, ever the practical one, got some blankets from the cupboard and wrapped them around Essie and Little Jim, whose teeth were chattering from fright and shock. They both looked so meek and small standing there in the middle of the living room. I wished I could do something to help them and hated feeling useless.

Papa guided them to the sofa while Grandpa went into the kitchen and warmed some milk and the coffee that Essie had made the day before, and served them to everyone in the living room.

Little Jim sat next to his mama on the sofa, still shivering and rocking back and forth. He kept saying, "The windows shattered...big crash...fire everywhere."

I took his puppy and gave him some warm milk, too. Then I sat down next to him and put my arms around him.

By that point, Essie had calmed enough to start telling us what she knew. From what we could piece together of her rambling words, the whole area of the Northern Quarters around their house was being shot up and burned to the ground. July had known that trouble was brewing. July Perry and his family were neighbors, and late in the afternoon, he'd told Big Jim, "I'm putting my gun in easy reach. Anybody that's got any wives or sweethearts better not come here bothering me. You better do the same."

Well, a group of armed white men did come and July was shot. Essie and Big Jim had heard him shouting for help to his oldest son and the two hired hands that were sleeping in the barn behind his house.

After the lull in the shooting, when it was discovered that two white men had been killed, the rest withdrew. Over Essie's objections, Big Jim had gone out to see what he could do to help. He'd come back and told them that he'd seen July's wife, Estelle, and their daughter Coretha crawling out the back of their house all the way to the cane break. He figured they were scared to stand up and run for fear of being killed. Jim wanted to call to them that they could hide in his house, but they were too far away, and he didn't want to draw attention to them. He didn't know if July had made it to safety.

Before long, white men arrived in horse-drawn wagons, Model Ts and trucks with torches and rifles. Big Jim saw the Orange County sheriff come in with a bunch of deputies. They first checked out July Perry's house only to discover that it was empty. When they started to search the surrounding cane fields Big Jim took off.

Soon, more men arrived and started to roam the streets of the Northern Quarters. When Big Jim came back to the house, he barricaded the front door with a wooden cabinet, and they all crouched down in a corner of the living room behind the dining table. Then they heard gunshots nearby and in the distance. At some point, rocks shattered the windows. There were people outside, laughing. Someone yelled, "We're gonna' burn us some niggers," and everyone cheered.

Then fiery torches flew in through the broken windows. They ignited the curtains and cushions on the sofa, and in no time the furniture was ablaze. By then Essie, Big Jim and Little

Jim were escaping out the back and hiding in the trees behind their yard. They stayed there, scared to death, watching their house being consumed by flames. When the rioters left, they came out and started to sneak away.

The sounds of gunshots and explosions near and far echoed in the night. Crackling bursts of sparks illuminated the sky as burning houses collapsed right before our eyes. The triumphant shouts and whooping of white men bent on destruction followed them as they made their way out of the neighborhood. When they saw roving gangs of rioters come down the streets with torches and guns, they quickly ducked behind trees and cowered in ditches until they had passed.

Walking through the backyard of one of the houses left standing, they heard a muffled cry for help come from inside. That's when Big Jim told Essie to go ahead with Little Jim and wait for him at our homestead.

As she got to that part, Essie's lips started to quiver violently and her eyes darted around the room.

To distract her, Papa asked, "What about your parents, Essie?"

She closed her eyes for a moment and let out a deep sigh. Then she said, more calmly, "They're safe. When we got the news of what happened to Mose, some of our neighbors took their wagons and left town as soon as darkness fell. We sent my parents with them."

"Why didn't you go, too?" Janie asked.

Essie looked at her, taken aback. "Why would we, child?" she said, her spirit reviving somewhat. "This is our home!"

We talked some more, but by then we were all spent, although sleep was out of the question. We were too wound up and worried. What a terrible time for all of us in Ocoee.

I continued to sit with Little Jim on the sofa, his puppy nuzzling between us. I must have dozed off a little, because when I was startled awake the early morning light was coming in through the window.

I realized there was a soft knocking at the back door. Everyone was on alert immediately. Papa got his rifle and went into the kitchen to look. We heard him exclaim, "Its Big Jim!"

Essie let out a cry of joy and leapt up from the sofa. Little Jim followed her. By then Big Jim was inside the living room. He looked exhausted, and there was a gash on his head, with blood on his cheek. He looked at Essie and said, "You're a sight for sore eyes, woman."

She gasped when she saw him, but he hugged her and put his arm around Little Jim. They stood that way for a long time with their eyes closed, swaying together, and we backed away to give them some privacy. Lizzie went into the kitchen and got a wet cloth.

When they finally joined us, Papa pulled out a chair from the dining room for Big Jim and said, "Let's have a look at that gash."

After examining it, he said, "It's not that bad, the cut isn't very deep."

Big Jim seemed embarrassed. "I don't even know how I got it," he said.

While Papa started to clean the wound and wrap a bandage around his head, Grandpa told Essie, "I'd much appreciate it if you would cook us all some breakfast." Big Jim started to get up, but Grandpa put a hand on his shoulder. "No, Big Jim, you stay right there at the table. It's all right."

Big Jim looked at him uncertainly, but then a glance passed between him and Essie, who gave him a slight nod, and he sat back. What was left of his energy drained out of him, and he looked completely worn out.

I must say that Essie outdid herself, fatigued as she must have been. We discovered how hungry we all were, putting away her biscuits, bacon, eggs, grits, and marmalade. It felt a bit awkward having our two families to share the same table, but it was all right. Big Jim looked downright funny with his head all covered with white gauze.

We kept the conversation to a minimum while we ate, but after we'd cleared the table, the adults started to talk about how to deal with the situation.

"Our house was one of the first to go," said Big Jim and shook his head in despair. "We've lost everything we had. There was no time to take anything with us, we just ran for our lives to get away from the fire, and now we don't even have a place to stay."

Essie looked up from her folded hands and said, "We could go to my sister's in Daytona Beach."

Grandpa, who had been pacing back and forth, stopped and said, "Big Jim, you know the Beulah property where we rotate the cows in the summer months?"

Big Jim replied, "Yes, Sir."

"On the back of the property is a little cottage that is well hidden among the trees. The three of you can lay low there until it's safe to leave for Daytona Beach."

Grandpa said to Essie, "Why don't you get some blankets and some food provisions from the kitchen to take with you?"

Then he got the shotgun from the front door and extra ammunition he had in the back closet and handed them to Big Jim so he could hunt the wild game on the property.

Papa got the truck to take them to the Beulah property. I wanted to give Essie and Little Jim a hug, but I could tell they were much too upset. I accompanied them out to the truck and heard Papa tell them to cover up with the blankets and keep quiet. Then he drove off and we got ready to go to the dairy and tend to the cows.

113

THE MASSACRE

Word about the battle at July Perry's house and the death of Leo Borgard and Elmer McDaniel traveled quickly. The official version, perpetrated by Colonel Salisbury and supported by others of his posse, was that a large gathering of armed blacks had opened fire unprovoked and killed two white men.

The more likely version, as related by Perry's daughter Coretha many years later, was that the two white men were killed by friendly fire because the posse surrounded the house without any plan or order and responded with indiscriminate gunfire after the initial shot. But Colonel Salisbury stuck to his account of being confronted by an army of angry blacks for the rest of his life.

The mere suggestion of an armed black uprising, struck fear and rage into the white population of all the surrounding towns. There was an electronic signboard in front of the newspaper office of the *Orlando Sentinel*, the first of its kind in the city. It was used to broadcast election returns from all over the area, and it alerted people to what had happened. Soon, carloads of angry white men raced to Ocoee to wreak vengeance.

Some of them were heard shouting, "Where are the goddam niggers?" and "I've come to kill a goddam nigger!"

Augmented by paramilitary vigilantes from Winter Garden and Apopka, two towns to the west and north of Ocoee, they surrounded the Northern Quarters. By the late evening other whites, many of them KKK members, came from as far away as Lakeland, Tampa, Arcadia and Jacksonville.

Orlando Sheriff Gordon deputized many of the men, giving official blessing to the ensuing riot.

They searched for July Perry in the cane field behind his house. He was well hidden, and one of the deputies almost stepped on him. Perry tried to shoot him, but the gun jammed and he was quickly overpowered. Perry was in bad shape. His left arm had been all but shot away, and he had lost a lot of blood. Some accounts describe him as being taken in the sheriff's car to the hospital in Orlando for medical treatment and from there to the county jail.

Meanwhile, in Ocoee, the white rioters went on a rampage through the Northern Quarters. They destroyed the black Masonic lodge and set fire to the two black churches. Explosions shook the ground. Some claimed they were from ammunition stored at one of the churches, others said they came when the burning houses collapsed. The area became a deadly inferno.

Black men, women and children were running everywhere, desperately hiding wherever they could—in trees and ditches, behind bushes, or in the fields. Many were injured as they tried to escape, getting shot, or suffering burns and scrapes and broken bones.

Some black residents fought back, and there were gun battles throughout the night, with the white attackers continuing to torch homes and driving the defenders into the surrounding woods, fields and swamp. They beat and castrated a black carpenter before killing him. Other victims were the wife and daughter of Will Edwards. They were shot trying to escape their burning home and ended up in the house. Roosevelt Barton perished in the barn on July Perry's property, where he'd been hiding, when the rioters set fire to Perry's homestead.

Altogether more than twenty houses were destroyed in the conflagration, virtually the whole black neighborhood. The only buildings left standing were the school house, which was on county property, and a barn believed to be owned by a white man.

Around 3:30 in the morning an angry mob of white vigilantes showed up at the jail, and the sheriff handed them the keys to Perry's cell. They hauled him out and dragged him behind a car to the neighborhood where Judge Cheney lived, north of the road leading to the Orlando Country Club. There, they lynched him by the entrance to the club, half a block away from the Judge's residence, as if to send a message to the Republican Senate candidate. Apparently, they used Perry for target practice, because when he was discovered hanging there the next morning, his lifeless body was riddled with bullets. Attached was a note proclaiming, "This is what we do to niggers who try to vote."

The next day J. B. Stone, a black undertaker, retrieved what was left of July Perry's body and buried him in a pauper's grave in Orlando's Greenwood Cemetery after the official inquest. The general public did not know the exact burial spot for years. At some point, Stone was visited by members of the KKK who told him that if he ever again took down a "cow" the whites had strung up, he would suffer the same fate.

The KKK's message was not lost on Judge Cheney. He called on the Orlando sheriff for protection and had armed guards standing outside his home for several days.

It was never determined how many African-American men women and children were murdered in the massacre. One of the reasons was that in the following days, many of the rioters and sightseers that traveled to Ocoee, sifted through the rubble and took away the charred bones of victims as souvenirs. Ultimately, only five deaths were officially confirmed.

The many blacks who hid in trees, bushes, and the nearby swamp until the mob dispersed, fled first to Winter Garden and Apopka, which both had sizable African American communities, and then beyond. By daylight, the Northern Quarters was a field of smoldering rubble and ruins of houses emptied of its former residents. Some were seen days later walking on the roads far away from the carnage, carrying nothing but the clothes on their back. None of them ever returned to Ocoee.

Perry's wife Estelle and daughter Coretha, who had been wounded by a gunshot, too, were ushered to safety by the authorities to Tampa and never charged with a crime.

No one knew what had happened to Mose Norman. The last time he'd been seen was after the incident at the polling station when he met the Reverend Franks on his way to the Northern Quarters, who bandaged his bleeding head. Some of the men from the posse that went to arrest July Perry looked for Mose at his house nearby, but didn't find him. He was never seen again in Ocoee and was presumed dead. However, during the night he got away and made a quick stop at Preacher Maxwell's house in Stuckey to say good-bye.

 He just drove out of town in his car and kept going. Some years later, it was discovered that he ended up in New York City, where he worked as a postal worker in Harlem until his death in 1949.

While Ocoee was by far the bloodiest retaliation white supremacists visited upon blacks who tried to exercise their right to vote, violence broke out in a number of other Florida communities as well. According to cautious estimates by the NAACP, which investigated the matter, between thirty and sixty African Americans had been murdered on Election Day and many more wounded throughout the state.

Although the deliberate violence and intimidation tactics succeeded in Ocoee and throughout Florida, which voted overwhelmingly for the Democrat Party, they could not prevent Warren G. Harding, a Republican, from becoming the 29th President of the United States.

But they reaped a bitter harvest, nonetheless. Not a single black vote was cast in elections in Orange County for the next 17 years.

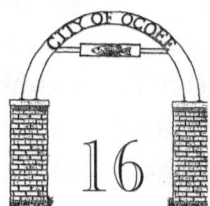

16

AFTERMATH

By the time we finished milking the cows; Eugene came by to reassure Janie that he was all right. His eyes were red-rimmed from lack of sleep and his face was drawn and haggard, but he was proud to have been deputized by Sheriff Gordon. He told the same story as Colonel Salisbury, that July Perry and a large contingent of Negroes holed up in his house had killed Leo Borgard and Elmer McDaniel. "They had fought like demons," he said. "It was horrible."

Except for the last part, I didn't believe a word he said. I figured, much as Ned was prone to exaggeration, I was more inclined to believe him and Big Jim for sure, that July Perry had been alone at home and was just trying to protect his family.

Janie fussed over Eugene. I was glad that he was all right, but also happy when he left to help patrol the Northern Quarters "to make sure all the newcomers streaming into town didn't cause any trouble." I wondered what he'd been doing all night.

When Papa came back with the Orlando newspaper, it told the same story, blaming everything on July Perry and lauding the white authorities for establishing law and order. I wasn't surprised that they got their facts wrong, claiming that it was July not Mose Norman who had arrived with a shotgun.

It went on to say that Perry had killed the two white men "in cold blood," but what was really odd was that the paper used the same phrase Eugene had, claiming that Perry's house was filled with armed Negroes who "fought like demons."

I doubt that the reporter had talked to Eugene, so that description came from someone else, higher up, and that they'd all agreed to fall in line and to use it to characterize what had happened and whitewashing their actions, so to speak.

I was exhausted, but it still made me angry!

While Papa and Grandpa went over to the burned out Northern Quarters north of Tullulah, I dozed off again. I was awake by the time they came back, shaking their heads in disbelief.

They had been allowed to go through the barricades by the armed guards Sheriff Gordon had deputized because they were Woodman of the World and were recognized as citizens of the area.

They got out of the truck and were shocked by all the smoldering ruins everywhere, homes and barns burnt to the ground. There were stray dogs. A terrible stench from the people and their livestock that had perished in the firestorm hung over the rubble and the fields. But what upset them the most was, when they got in the truck to leave, they spotted people who had come from out of town and were gathering souvenirs. One man was laughing as he held up bones of Negroes that had been burned while others were there with cameras taking pictures of all the destruction. In fact, pictures of July Perry and the cane field where he was caught were sold for twenty-five cents. They were placed in several stores for all to see.

Then we made our rounds to deliver milk. When we got to Mrs. Carrington's, I took the opportunity to let her know that I was collecting clothing and blankets for the poor and needy in the area. Mrs. Carrington always was a kind, generous woman, and she took the time to find a shawl, some dresses and two blankets to donate to the cause. I thanked her, and told her they would be put to good use.

When we were back in the truck, Papa said, "That was smart thinking, Georgia. Now we can take the clothes and blankets out to Essie and Big Jim."

Thursday afternoon I went with Grandpa to the Beulah property. I took some food provisions and the clothing that I had collected. As we drove down the two-lane dirt path that led to the cottage, Grandpa said, "We will take them to Daytona Beach on Sunday morning. We think the time is right."

I hoped all would go well for my dear friends. When we came to the cottage I jumped out and ran ahead. As I came up to the door, I heard Essie and Little Jim singing inside:

Fry the meat—you give me the skin,
and that's where all of our troubles begin.

I recognized the Juba song, but then Grandpa slammed the door to the truck and the singing inside stopped immediately. Little Jim carefully peeked out from one of the windows.

But it was Big Jim who opened the door, carrying the shotgun, a worried expression on his face. He still had a bandage on his forehead. When he saw us, he relaxed a bit.

Essie called from inside, "Come on in, child."

I said, "Let me get what we brought you first," and headed back to the truck. When Little Jim joined me, his puppy gamboling alongside, I asked, "Little Jim how are you?"

He said, "I'm OK, but I'm lonesome. My Daddy has been hunting rabbits and finding cooters, so we have had plenty to eat. Ya know, my Mama can make a delicious meal out of nothing." "She made us a great mess of greens and corn bread last night for supper." I thought, wish I had been there.

"I heard you singing the Juba song when we came."

Little Jim nodded and smiled. "We've been making up new verses," he said.

From the back of the truck, I loaded him up with flour, fat back, a few eggs, and some cans of beans.

Grandpa was talking to Essie and Big Jim and they were listening to him seriously. "The whole Northern Quarters has cleared out and is being patrolled by the men the sheriff deputized. Given the mood in town, it simply isn't safe for you here. I don't even know if it makes sense to come back at a later time."

"But this is our home," Essie protested. "Little Jim has grown up here."

When they realized I was there they stopped their talking.

I held out the clothes to Essie and said, "These are from Mrs. Carrington."

She gave me an odd look, but took them and put them on a chair by the table. In a minute she held up one of the dresses, clasped it to her chest and smoothed out the plaid skirt over hers. The first smile I'd seen from her in days appeared on her face, and she said, "This will fit me just fine."

"It will be good to have when you get to Daytona Beach."

"Yes," she said, but her sad expression returned.

To cheer her up a bit, Big Jim said," Essie, you will be as pretty as gals goin' to meetings over yonder in Daytona."

Essie gave him a slight smile then.

While Little Jim and I played outside with his puppy, Grandpa continued to talk to his parents inside. Through the door, I could see Essie and Big Jim listening with their lips pressed together. They didn't say a word.

At some point, Grandpa said, "We need to leave. We don't want to be gone too long." He added, "Big Jim, we'll be here Sunday morning to get an early start."

I had tears in my eyes as we drove away, but I was thankful that my dear friends had a safe place to go.

Over the next few days, much was made of Ocoee's Election Day massacre in the newspapers. One story praising the whites told of Mr. Wells, a grocer, opening up his store during the riot, making sandwiches and serving coffee for the vigilantes that were destroying the Northern Quarters. There were accounts of the Negroes running and hiding in the woods all night while houses burned to the ground before their eyes.

When we drove around to make deliveries, we saw armed guards patrolling the streets of the town. The houses of white folks close to the Southern Quarters had their window shades drawn and many a woman of the house first peeked cautiously through the blinds before opening the front doors to receive their milk and eggs from us. They were visibly relieved. Several told us that they were frightened to death of the Negroes retaliating against them and their families.

People who showed up at the dairy shared stories, too. I had to bite my lips when some of the men bragged about how they made sure that none of the violence spilled over into the white sections of town and opined that "The niggers got exactly what they deserved!"

I'd start to softly hum the Juba song to myself in protest and to drown out their voices.

Newspaper coverage in Florida of the event was uniformly pro-white and often provided lurid and trumped up details. *The Tampa Tribune* described July Perry as a troublemaker, a violent man who had perhaps killed one or two Negroes, "but has always escaped on a self-defense plea." It also reported that, "Between 500 and 1,000 rounds of ammunition exploded in the church and Perry's house, where they congregated and desperate blacks fought like demons," suggesting that the firestorm was caused by the black inhabitants.

The Florida Metropolis, a Jacksonville paper, opined that the black quarters in Ocoee were the refuge of armed Negroes who offered resistance and had to be burned out, exonerating the white vigilantes of any responsibility for starting the fires that engulfed the neighborhood.

In the meantime, there was an inquest into the deaths of the two white men, Leo Borgard and Elmer McDaniel, who were widely portrayed as heroes and victims. They'd fought in World War I and had worn parts of their uniforms in the fatal encounter. A coroner's jury concluded that their deaths occurred at 9 p.m. and resulted from the shots that came from Perry's house. "This verdict is borne out by the evidence that Perry's house was filled with armed Negroes planning a disturbance in the community," their report claimed. No mention was made of the fact that both men had belonged to the Ku Klux Klan. Nor was any other evidence considered of what happened besides Colonel Salisbury's account, which was echoed by all the other participants of the posse.

The funeral service for Leo Borgard was held in the Winter Garden Methodist Church the Friday after the massacre under the direction of the Masonic Order. According to the Orlando Morning Sentinel, it was one of the largest funerals ever held there. All the nearby streets were closed to traffic because of the size of the crowds of people before and after the service.

Borgard's body was buried in the Oakland Cemetery. The large gravestone, five feet high, a monument to white supremacy, is still standing. It is engraved both with Masonic symbols up top and the KKK motto "Non Silba Sed Anthar (Not Self, but Others)." A frieze below, sandwiched by the two words "Duty" and "Honor," shows two Klan nightriders in robes, their horses rearing up and pawing the air. Beneath it is the phrase "Only the American Stands on Guard." There is a smaller gravestone behind it with Borgard's name and "Florida Corp 336" engraved on it.

The family of Elmer McDaniel held a smaller service at a Winter Garden funeral home with the same pastor who had officiated at Borgard's funeral. Afterwards, McDaniel's brother and his wife took the body by train back to Georgia where he was originally from. They buried him with honors at Stone Mountain, where the KKK had been reborn just five years earlier, as a martyr to the cause.

The African Americans killed in the riot remained nameless, although they all showed signs of having been shot and burned. Carey Hand Funeral Home in Orlando sent a hearse to pick up the bodies and they were interred together in an unknown grave site at the County's expense. The identity of the Negroes and the location of their grave is still unknown today.

An editorial in the *Orlando Evening Reporter-Star* opined, "Now that the disturbance in the western section of the county has come to an end, all citizens should forget it as soon as possible."

An editorial from the *Deland News* laid the blame for the massacre at the doorstep of Orlando Republicans:

> *The sympathy of the News goes out to the poor unfortunate negroes who were shot down in Orange County this week. They were only pawns in the game. The entire blame for their murder rests upon the white skunks who put them up to voting, and made them believe that they were just as good as white men and*

women.... The blood of the murdered negroes is on the heads of these carpetbaggers who protected themselves with the naked bodies of the inferior race.

A month later, a Grand Jury was convened in Orlando to investigate the incident. All of the whites, including KKK members, known to have participated were subpoenaed, but no action was taken against them. After all, the sheriff and his deputies belonged to the Klan, as did members of the Grand Jury. No wonder, they concluded:

Sheriff Frank Gordon and his deputies...the members of Orlando Memorial Post No. 09, American Legion, together with other ex-service men, and the leading citizens of Ocoee, Winter Garden, Orlando and other nearby towns have performed their full duty in maintaining law and order...and admirably succeeded in the execution of their obligations as loyal American citizens.

But that was not enough to whitewash what had happened. At some point, someone made a revision in July Perry's death certificate. The black undertaker had written "By being Hung" as the cause of death. Sometime later another person added "not by violence caused by racial disturbance." This feeble attempt to gloss over what really happened was as transparent as it was ineffective.

17

THE VANISHING

Miss Darla Dream, one of Grandpa's oldest friends stopped by the dairy toward the end of the week. She was a kind-hearted woman, a spinster who had lived in Ocoee all her life. Although at least twenty years younger, she had taken a shine to him and visited often to say hello and see how he was doing. She told Grandpa that she and others in Ocoee were still scared to death. If it weren't for the armed men patrolling the streets day and night, she would fear for her life. All of the women and children stayed inside their houses with the window shades drawn.

Darla had just come from visiting Mrs. Gordon's house close to the Southern Quarters, where some of the black families that lived there had come back after the riot. She wanted to check up on her and make sure she was safe. She had coffee and toast with Mrs. Gordon and one of her neighbors, Mrs. Helmley. Both ladies were visibly shaken. Darla related their conversation.

According to Mrs. Helmley, "One of the nigger families that returned to their home east of town found it had been bombed. The family left Ocoee immediately."

Then Mrs. Gordon weighed in, "I don't understand why some of the whites are trying to get the niggers to stay on. They're not welcome here anymore."

"Once they saw the cardboard skeletons hanging on the porch rafters of their homes, they got the message," Mrs. Gordon said.

It made me worry about Essie, Big Jim and Little Jim being in danger all alone in a cottage in the middle of nowhere. I hoped they were safe.

After Darla left Grandpa mentioned that some kind of committee was being formed to compensate the Negroes who were leaving their property. Captain Sims was in charge, and Eugene's father, Mr. Pike was on it, too.

"They asked me to join, told me I could double my land at bargain prices, but I want nothing to do with it," he scoffed.

Papa agreed with him. "We don't want to profit from the misery that has been afflicted on others."

It was one of the few times during those horrible days when I felt good for a moment. I was proud of Papa and Grandpa.

Sunday morning Lizzie and I got up and made sausage biscuits and a crock of sweet tea and packed them in our picnic basket.

Papa's eyes lit up and he said, "When we get to the cattle crossing in Deland, that lunch sure will taste good."

There were patches of fog on the ground when we all piled into the truck, even Janie, and drove to the Beulah property. Along the way, Grandpa said to Papa, "Be careful and go the back way into Deland, then over to the coast. Once you get to Deland you're in Volusia County, so you can rest a little easier."

Papa said, "Don't worry I know my way around the back roads."

When we got to the cottage, Essie, Big and Little Jim were already waiting outside. They had their meager belongings in a crocker sack, and Little Jim was holding his puppy in his arms. I was glad they were all right.

Grandpa went inside, returned with the blankets and held them out to Essie. "Take them, it'll get chilly on the back of the truck, and you'll need them when it gets cold this winter."

Big Jim said, "We're much obliged, Mr. Kambel. We can't thank you enough for what you've done for us."

Grandpa actually blushed and said, "What are friends for if not to help in times of need."

When Big Jim held out the shotgun to him, he said, "Take it with you, just in case. My son can bring it back with him."

We all stood around awkwardly, dreading what would come next. Papa broke the mood by saying, "Well, we've got to get going."

Lizzie and Janie nodded glumly and went to Big Jim's family. They shook his hand and got a hug from Essie. Little Jim stood there, rocking, holding on to his puppy, and my sisters gave him an awkward hug, too. I was rooted to the spot, unable to move.

Finally, Essie said, "Georgia, come here."

I ran to her and threw myself into her arms, sobbing, "Oh, Essie, I don't want you to go."

Essie comforted me for a spell. Finally, she pushed me away and said, "Now, child, you stay strong." Then she drew me to her again and whispered in my ear, "I don't want Little Jim to lose his composure."

I nodded and dried my eyes. She looked at me with so much love I almost burst into tears again. She kissed me on the cheek and said, "Be well, Georgia. God willing, we will see each other again."

Then she turned away, hugged Grandpa, nodded to Papa and climbed in the back of the truck.

I shook Big Jim's hands, my small hands disappearing in his big paws. Then I went to Little Jim and said, "Take good care of that puppy, Little Jim. I'll pray for you."

"Me, too," he said in a barely audible voice, his eyes tearing up.

I embraced him and he handed me the puppy to hold while he joined his mama. I felt its breath quicken in my arms. It was sensing our sadness and was getting upset, too. I turned quickly to hide my quivering lips.

The last to climb aboard was Big Jim. Papa handed him and Essie a bunch of blankets, reached the puppy up to Little Jim, and waited until they all got comfortable. Then he and Grandpa covered them with a big tarp and weighed it down with some bricks. They didn't want to take the risk of someone along the way recognizing the family and causing trouble.

Papa got in front, shifted into first gear and slowly drove down the path. Even though Essie, Big Jim and Little Jim couldn't see us, we waved after them until the truck was just a little dot in the distance.

I went inside the cottage because I wasn't ready to go home yet. I was hoping that Essie had left something behind I could take with me to remember her by, but it was neat as a pin. It looked like she and her family had never been there.

I didn't hear Grandpa come up next to me until he put his arm around my shoulder and said, "Come, Georgia. We've got to get back to the dairy."

He locked up, and we all walked through the fields in silence. The morning sun had burned the mist away and the rays warmed my face, but I felt cold and forlorn inside. I didn't know if I would ever see Essie, Big Jim or Little Jim again.

It turned out to be a long Sunday. I could not get my mind off Papa, although I knew he could take care of himself and any situation that might come up. I kept saying prayers for him, Big Jim, Essie, and Little Jim. I knew God was with them and would protect them. Lizzie, Janie and I took care of the chores. Grandpa and Sarah were busy herding the cows in for milking.

We were very short handed and everyone was busy getting the milk ready for the dairy store.

There still were a lot of people from other places in town since the riot, and they came by in the afternoon and bought all the milk, especially Papa's chocolate milk that disappeared as quickly as Sarah could get the shelves stocked. I thought to myself, "We certainly won't need the ice that Abner the ice man had brought to the store that morning."

At some point, Eugene came by and picked up Janie in his car to go to dinner at his parents' house. It was getting late so Lizzie and I asked Grandpa if we could walk home. He said, "No, you better wait for me because, there's so many new people around that we don't know."

It took him a while to finish up and by the time we got back to the homestead the sun was setting.

Lizzie and I prepared supper and as we were about to finish, we heard the truck pull up. It was Papa! Lizzie and I ran out to greet him with big hugs and bombarded him with questions.

He smiled and said, "Just wait until I get inside and get something to eat. I'm starving."

Grandpa, watching from the front porch said, "Girls get the plates on the table and let's have some supper."

As we ate hungrily, Papa told us that the trip had gone without a hitch. Once they were past Lake Monroe and Deland, Papa stopped and took the tarp off and they all had an early lunch, then he had Essie and Little Jim sit in the truck's cabin next to him. When they got to Daytona Beach, they drove to Mrs. Bethune's school because everyone who works there has to go to chapel with the girls. Essie went inside to find her sister. Louise was so glad to see her and Big and Little Jim. She had heard the terrible news from Ocoee and had worried herself sick about them. She told them that

Essie's parents had arrived earlier in the week, all safe and sound, and they'd be so happy to see them.

Louise asked Papa if he would take them the two blocks to her house. When they got there, Little Jim and his puppy jumped out, as if they knew they were home.

Papa ended his account, saying, "Big Jim and Essie came over and thanked me again for everything. We said our good-byes and I got on the road to Deland. It was a solemn ride home, but Essie, Big Jim, and Little Jim are finally safe."

I was glad to hear that, but it didn't heal the sorrow in my heart.

The next evening, Eugene came by the house for supper. He and Janie had started to talk about getting married in June and all the preparations they'd have to make. I was glad for Janie. At least one person in our house had some happiness. But then Eugene started to talk about how he and his daddy had acquired some fine farmland for vegetables and several groves that had belonged to some of the black families in the Southern and Northern Quarters. "We just about doubled our holdings. Got the land at fire sale prices," he bragged, with no inkling what he was saying, considering people had burned to death in the massacre.

When Janie chimed in, "Isn't it wonderful?" Papa and Grandpa exchanged a glance and concentrated on eating their food.

But something boiled over inside me. I jumped out of my chair and threw down my napkin. "You should be ashamed of yourselves," I yelled. "Essie and Big Jim and Little Jim did nothing wrong and you'all burned down their home, and now you're both acting like nothing happened and reveling in your good fortune. But it has come at the cost of other people's suffering. You disgust me!"

Then I ran to the sleeping porch because I didn't want them to see me cry. I sat hunched over on my bed in the dark, sobbing for a long time, until Papa came in.

He stood by the door for a moment, a shadowy figure. Then he started in a soft, voice, "Now, Georgia, I know you're upset. We all are. But that is no way to talk to your sister and our guest. Come and say you're sorry. Tell them you didn't mean it."

I gritted my teeth and spat out, "No, I won't. I meant every word."

Papa waited a spell. Then he said with exasperation and sadness in his voice, "Well, until you apologize, you are not welcome at the table."

He left and I felt miserable and abandoned. I looked out the window over Starke Lake and watched the moonlight dance on the swells. I wanted to cry out in anger and rage, but remained silent. I had no more tears.

After the destruction of the Northern Quarters, many of the African Americans in the Southern Quarters decided to leave, too. Those who remained were intimidated and hounded until they too, made themselves scarce. In addition to the cardboard skeletons the white owners hung up to scare their black tenants, they threatened to shoot them or burn their homes if they did not get out.

Walter White, the assistant secretary of the NAACP, came to Ocoee soon after the riot to investigate what had happened. He was light-skinned enough to pass for white and found that many of the whites were "still giddy with victory." Their attitude was that they had done a good job in preventing the inferior Negroes from voting and acting like equals of their betters.

The committee of "responsible whites" appointed to help the departing blacks who owned property, paid cents on the dollar for some of the most fertile land in the area. Later, when there were questions about the sales, the committee members claimed that the Negroes had received reasonable compensation.

Considering how many whites enriched themselves at the expense of the African Americans whose homes had been destroyed, it is not far-fetched to say that many of Ocoee's whites used the spark that had originated at the voting station and grown into a conflagration to take revenge on the successful, "uppity" blacks like July Perry and Mose Norman. Then they used the pretext of the massacre to drive the remaining blacks out.

In his report, Walter White described what he saw:

At the time that I visited Ocoee, the last colored family of Ocoee was leaving with their goods piled high on a motor truck with six colored children on top. White children stood around and jeered the Negroes who were leaving, threatening them with burning if they did not jury up and get away. These children thought it a huge joke that some Negroes had been burned alive.

Altogether about 500 African Americans were driven out of Ocoee. For years the only black resident remaining in town was Burley Jones, the ex-slave of Mr. Sims, who had warned the whites that the Negroes were threatening to make trouble. He lived there until he was too old to take care of himself and ended up in the County nursing home paid for by some Ocoee citizens.

After that Ocoee became a lily-white place, a "sunset town" where no African Americans dared to show their faces after dark.

ANOTHER WEDDING

I made my peace with Janie a day later and told her I was sorry. She made it easy for me, saying I didn't have to mention it, that we were all wound tight as a tick and, as far as she was concerned, it was water under the bridge. When I gave a half-hearted apology to Eugene, he accepted it graciously, but he never warmed up to me again and treated me with polite formality. Not that I cared.

Over the following weeks, a quiet sadness set in around our house. No more Essie, Big Jim, and Little Jim coming to work and play, no more delicious meals cooked by Essie. We all tried our best, but we didn't feel like we were "living in high cotton" any longer.

At the dairy, the men who came to pick up milk and eggs told that their wives complained that they no longer had blacks to do household chores, and had to cook their own meals and take care of their small children. At our house, those tasks fell to Janie, Lizzie and me. It turned out that Lizzie was a surprisingly good cook. She must have been watching and learning from Essie more than I realized.

By then, all of the blacks from the Southern Quarters were gone, too.

Every available white man was working in the fields and groves, harvesting the orange crop and vegetables. Some had reached out to black workers in the Orlando, Winter Garden and Apopka communities, but after what happened on Election Day, none of them wanted to set foot in Ocoee.

By Thanksgiving, most of the outsiders had gone home and the local men stopped patrolling the streets. School resumed and life supposedly returned to normal. Everyone acted like nothing had happened.

One day, I decided to go to the Northern Quarters after school, to see the devastation for myself. With the harvest, no one had the time to clear the rubble away, and the charred remains of wooden timbers lay everywhere. I walked past the ruins of July Perry's house to Big Jim's and Essie's homestead. The stone foundation supports were still in place and visible between the burnt timbers, indicating the outline of what had been their house.

I had a lump of pain in my chest the whole time.

At some point, an older white man with cotton-white hair I didn't know came out of one of the houses that was still standing and called out to me from the porch, "What are you doing here? Are you lost?"

I said, "No, I'm all right. I just wanted to see."

As he came down the steps toward me, I became afraid, but then I recognized him as one of Grandpa's Woodmen of the World friends and relaxed.

He said, "You're Ed Kambel's daughter, ain't ya, Georgia?"

"Yes."

He shook his head. "Terrible what happened here, just terrible."

He was the first white man I heard express any regret out loud. The only ones who'd piped up until then were mighty proud of what they'd done, whether they'd participated or just stood by as their black neighbors were burned and hounded out of town. I knew there were rumors that a few whites had harbored and protected some of the black refugees and helped them get to safety, just like Papa and Grandpa. But I can't imagine there were many, and no one talked about that.

The man looked at me intently and said, "This is no place for you, girl. You better get on home."

I did a quick curtsy and left as fast as I could. It was the last time I set foot in the Northern Quarters.

One Saturday morning close to Christmas, Janie said, "Girls, I will not be at the dairy today. Eugene and I have our wedding plans to discuss."

Lizzie and I just looked at her. Although David had returned from his patrolling duties, we were still short-handed.

I said, "We have not had a day off since the riot, and I don't know when we will get one. We can't seem to get enough milk ready for the day."

Janie didn't even seem to hear me. "Mrs. Pike wants to talk about my wedding dress!"

She was so excited. I didn't want to burst her bubble, even though I felt resentful, so I didn't say anymore. It would not do any good any way.

Lizzie and I went to the dairy and started our daily chores. Sarah, who was already there putting out fresh eggs, mentioned that she and David would be going to a dance in Montverde that night. A square dance caller was coming into town from Eustis, and several couples from Ocoee were going with them. I knew they would enjoy it and wished I had someone to take me.

The day passed by very slowly. After the second milking in the late afternoon, Papa said that we could go home. Shortly after we got there, Janie came rushing into the house.

"Eugene and I have set a date for our wedding in May," she announced triumphantly. "I would have liked it to be right after Christmas, but he and his daddy have a lot on their hands with all their new land." She hardly took a breath before going on. "I will be wearing Mrs. Pike's wedding dress. It fits me perfectly. Georgia, you will be my maid of honor, and David will be Eugene's best man."

It was her way of extending an olive branch, and I should have been pleased that she chose me rather than Lizzie who, after all, was a year older than me. But I just looked at her and said, "OK, what do I wear?"

"Mrs. Pike said we will have a mint green dress made for you and she knows the perfect dressmaker. Next week we will go select the fabric, because we only have a few months to get everything ready and time flies."

I really missed Essie then. She would have made my dress, and it would have been beautiful. I started to think about her and Big Jim and Little Jim and how they were doing. I wondered if I would ever get to see them again.

Next week came and when it was time to select the fabric, Eugene drove us to a fancy dress shop in Orlando, acting quite the gentleman. Janie found a mint green satin she liked. "That color will look pretty next to my gown."

I didn't really care and was just going through the motions. I did not feel like being in a wedding, but Janie was so excited I just went along with her. I had to admit, the fabric was lovely, and Mrs. Pike was buying it and having my dress made. So I said, "I'm sure that everything will be beautiful."

We continued to work long hours at the dairy with no end in sight. And we were not alone. Everyone in town was doing double duty because so many Negro workers had been driven away.

But time passed and before long it was May and the day of Janie's and Eugene's wedding.

When we got up that morning, Janie was excited and talking a mile a minute. She took forever to get dressed, however, even with Lizzie's help, so I came out in my new brides maid outfit first, and Papa and Grandpa said I looked very lovely. I felt embarrassed and wished Essie was there to reassure me.

Then Janie walked out of the bedroom in her wedding dress, Lizzie holding her train, and all eyes were on her.

Papa hugged her and said, "You look beautiful."

She really did, I had to admit. Papa and Grandpa looked nice, too, in their suits, and Lizzie wore her Sunday dress. When we were all ready, we got in the car Mr. Pike had sent for us and headed over to the Christian Church.

When we arrived, I went inside and walked to the altar area where Eugene and David, his best man, were already standing. Grandpa and Lizzie took their seats. Mr. and Mrs. Pike craned their necks expectantly as Papa escorted Janie looking radiant down the aisle. She carried a bouquet of white roses, from Mrs. Carrington's rose garden and handed them to me.

Then Papa put Janie's hand in Eugene's. I looked at the two of them standing in front of the pastor and did hope they would be happy together. The pastor said some words about what it takes to make a successful marriage and, after they said their vows, pronounced them husband and wife. They kissed and left the Church smiling and everyone was invited to the reception hall for cake and punch.

It wasn't as lavish as Charlotte Ann's—there weren't any important guests from up north—but the Pikes had spared no expense. Most of the attendees were friends of theirs, members of the Ocoee, Winter Garden and Oakland elite. Although I spent time with David because he was the best man, it was awkward and formal, and he wasted no time looking for his precious Sarah.

Ned was there with his parents and sisters, but I didn't feel like listening to him and avoided him. Lizzie took pity on him, however, and sat and talked with him for a while.

When it was time for the bridal couple to leave for their newly built house on the Pike farm land, a gift from Eugene's parents, Janie was still glowing.

Soon after, Papa, Grandpa, Lizzie and I left for our home-stead. Everyone was quiet on the way home, and we were happy to relax for the evening and go to sleep, to be rested before the early morning chores started again.

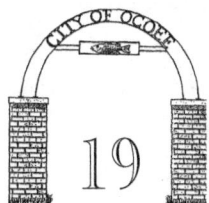

FISH CAMP

Life had been toil and work for a long while, so we were excited when Papa told us that Ned's folks had invited us over to their camp house for a fish fry on Sunday. He said for Lizzie and me to bring our swim suits since the weather would be warm. Grandpa would stay behind, and Sarah and David would get their families to pitch in so we could take the time off from the dairy.

We took some sweet cream and butter along for Ned's Mom and headed out on Lakewood, the main road out of Ocoee to the east. It was a short drive, and when we arrived, I could smell the fish and hushpuppies that were already frying. Ned told us to hurry and put our suits on because he was going to row us out to the center of Starke Lake in the bass boat. I was nervous, knowing from experience we couldn't trust Ned not to play a prank of some kind, but what could go wrong in the middle of the lake?

So we changed in the house. I had a dark brown top with sleeves and matching pants that came to just above my knees and Lizzie wore a black one-piece outfit that covered her arms to the elbows and her knees. Ned had on a two piece, blue-and-white striped suit and wore a straw boater. He did all the rowing until we got to the middle of the lake. It was a calm, sunny day, and I enjoyed being out on the water.

Ned pulled in the oars. Then he laughed and said, "You ladies are going to dive for nigger bones today."

I was bewildered. What did that mean? I had heard kids at school say it, but didn't give it much thought.

Ned explained, "Some of the niggers from the massacre got thrown in the lake, or at least their bones. I'm going to dive first to show you how it's done."

He jumped in, rocking the boat and treaded water for a moment. Then he went under head first and stayed down a long time. He finally came up and, taking big gulps of air and splashing around, said, "No Luck, Now your turn Georgia."

I gave him a look like he was some vile kind of insect and said, "No. I refuse."

While he called to Lizzie to join him, I put in the oars and started to row back. He finally climbed in the boat and took over from me as if nothing had happened.

When we returned, I ran to the house and changed into my dry clothes. Then it was time for supper. I was hungry and the smells made my mouth water. As I went to get a plate, there was Ned standing close by.

He grinned and announced loudly for all to hear, "I took the Kambel girls diving for nigger bones!"

Some of the men and women chuckled, but I was horrified. I just wanted to die right on the spot. Lizzie didn't look very happy either. I wanted to go home without eating, but it would have been rude, so we stayed a while longer.

Finally, we left. In the truck on the way back, Papa said, "I'm sorry that happened at supper. That boy has no sense."

I said, "He could use a good thrashing."

For the rest of the ride, we all remained silent. I didn't ever want to see Ned again.

∽

At that point, G'ma's journal breaks off except for a few brief entries, as if she didn't want to think anymore about all that had happened. In a community where so many people had participated in driving away the African American population and were either proud of that fact or wanted to forget it, she must have felt like a complete outsider. I imagine her humming the Juba song to herself most of the time.

G'ma wrote a single sentence acknowledging that she graduated from school in 1923, but she had nothing to say about what else happened to her that year. On November 24, sixty-five men and women who were qualified to vote met at the J.R. Pounds Packing House. They selected officers and organized a municipal government to incorporate a territory of three square miles as the "Town of Ocoee."

By then, Ocoee had a population of 450, electric lights, water works, hotels, two diners, two dry good stores, a physician, a post master, a real estate office, and an agent for the two railroads that went through town.

But things continued to be difficult for Ocoee's residents. In retrospect, it's hard to separate how much that was due to the massacre and its aftermath or the bottom dropping out of the land boom, which brought the Great Depression to Florida four years earlier than to the rest of the United States.

In any case, it didn't take long for the town leaders to realize that money was needed for improvement projects like brick paving the main roads and putting in water and electricity systems. When they discovered that they could borrow the funds from the State of Florida and levy local taxes to repay the loans, they applied to have the municipal government abolished and be reinstated as "The City of Ocoee."

The State granted the request and the change took place on May 13, 1925. One of the first pieces of legislation passed by the city fathers was to call for the construction of two gates at the northern and southern entrances to Ocoee.

It made G'ma so angry that she wrote the words that got me interested in her journal:

> Last week, Ocoee became its own city, with two brand-new city gates and not a word about the massacre that occurred just a few years back and the bad things that have happened since then, so I am going to write about it, even if no one wants to talk about it.

The southern arch was an iron half circle with "City of Ocoee" inside two parallel, curved rods with a large-mouth bass hanging below. They were mounted on two brick covered columns that stood on either side of Bluford Avenue. On the back of the arch was written the word "Mizpah," which comes from the Old Testament, Genesis 31:49, and means, "May the Lord watch between you and me when we are absent one from the other." It was a surprising wish for anyone departing from Ocoee, considering what had happened to its African-American inhabitants.

In another entry, G'ma commented:

> It was very hard to understand why they put up that sign since so many people had been run off, burned out, or killed. The town was called a "white capped" town now. This meant the entire black communities had been razed to the ground in order to "purify" the area for whites. To me it meant that Essie, Big Jim and Little Jim will never come to our house again.

I suspect that when she visited in 1934 to attend the funeral of Papa, she must have felt a certain satisfaction to learn that the northern arch had been razed two years earlier because it kept getting hit by cars. The southern gate was torn down in 1940 for the same reason.

In the meantime, there was one more long entry, and I was very happy to read it.

20

VERNON

The drudgery of working at the dairy took its toll on me. I also felt alone and unhappy most of the time, living in a place I didn't like anymore and where I couldn't respect anyone but Papa and Grandpa; nor could I see any way out of my predicament.

The Pikes and other families were thriving even during the leaner times, in part because of all the land they'd gotten from the Negro families that had been run out of town. We didn't see a whole lot of Janie after she got married. I'll say one thing for her and Eugene, though. They never turned their backs on us, now that we were their poor relations. Lizzie and me were always included in the social events.

One such special event was a Labor Day picnic held by Mrs. Carrington when her daughter and husband came for a visit. Charlotte Ann and Colonel Duckworth would spend Christmas in Washington. This was the only other time he got off from the military. Lizzie didn't want to go at first because Ned hadn't been invited, but she finally gave in.

To my amazement and horror, she and Ned had started to see each other, going to dances together. I hated having him come by more often. But when I finally had enough and challenged her about it, Lizzie simply said, "What other options do

I have? I'm not beautiful like Janie or pretty like you." I didn't have an answer for that.

On Saturday morning before Labor Day, Lizzie and I got up early and went to the dairy so we could get our chores done. Then we hurried home and got dressed in our finest outfits just in time for Janie and Eugene to pick us up. Janie was excited about seeing Charlotte Ann again, and she was dressed up, fit to kill. She liked to show off her fancy new clothes that Eugene bought for her.

It was a hot September day and I was glad Eugene had the top down, although it meant Lizzie and me, in back, had to hold on to our hair because of the breeze. As we approached the Oak Hill Mansion and turned into the large gates we saw several of the Negro grounds keepers working in the distance down by Lake Apopka. It was a strange sight, because we hadn't seen any black faces in Ocoee since the massacre. I felt a pang and thought of Essie, Big Jim and Little Jim again. I continued to miss them and prayed every day that they were doing well.

Eugene drove his shiny car up the winding driveway lined by oak trees dripping with Spanish moss and let us out at the front entrance to the mansion. While he parked, Charlotte Ann rushed out to greet us like she'd been waiting all morning for us to show up. She was pregnant again and had that special glow that expectant mothers have. She and Janie fell into each other's arms and started to chatter away. Meanwhile, Mrs. Carrington came out smiling and said that she was glad to see us, and ushered Lizzie and me in to the big front room.

I recognized a number of the local guests, but there were others I didn't—friends of the hosts from out of town. Among them were Mr. and Mrs. R. J. Reynolds, a handsome couple from Virginia. They were gracious when Mrs. Carrington introduced us, but I barely paid attention because next to them stood a tall, young man. He had a tanned complexion, penetrating blue eyes, and soft features. We looked at each other, and time seemed to stand still.

I just caught his name, Vernon, when Mrs. Carrington made the introductions.

He bowed smartly and said, "Pleased to meet you, Georgia. May I escort you to the picnic grounds?"

I nodded and offered him my arm. As we sauntered outside he told me that he worked for Mr. Reynolds, who owned a large tobacco business. "My parents died when I was young, and the Reynolds took me under their wing. I'm very grateful to them."

We got chicken and corn from the picnic tables and took our plates down to the lake, where we sat on a big oak log at the water's edge. Vernon started to enjoy the corn, but I only picked at my food.

He said, "Georgia, you aren't hungry? This is the best corn I've ever tasted."

I flushed and shook my head. I liked listening to his voice as he told me about his work and how beautiful Virginia was.

When we finished our lunch, we took a walk together along Lake Apopka. Vernon spoke about his job at the Reynolds Tobacco Company. When I told him about working at the dairy, he wanted to know all about the things that I had to do every day. Then we headed back to the picnic area for dessert, hand churned peach ice cream, my favorite.

Mr. and Mrs. Carrington and the Reynolds were playing a game of croquet. Lizzie was sitting in the swing with Jasper, the Carrington's hound dog at her side. Eugene and Janie were out on the lake in a boat with Charlotte Ann and Duck.

I decided to show Vernon the Carrington's azalea and rose gardens on the other side of the property. "I love roses," I told him.

He asked, "What is your favorite color?"

"Pink."

"That color suits you."

When we got there, he plucked a pink rose bud from one of the bushes and placed it in my hair. I had never blushed before, but my checks were bright pink. He looked down at me and kissed me. My heart started to pound in my chest, and my checks felt like they were burning and glowing.

As we went back, he said, "We're leaving tomorrow after church, Georgia, but I'd like to see you again on my next visit. In the meantime, will you write to me?"

I said, "Yes, Vernon, I will."

Eugene and Janie returned from their boating trip and it was time to say our good-byes. Vernon and I looked at each other and Vernon said that he would be back for a visit as soon as he could, but please write to me Georgia. I promise I will. Then everyone thanked the Carrington's for a lovely picnic.

On the ride home Eugene said, "Well, it looks like Georgia and Vernon really hit it off."

Janie agreed with him. I remained silent, lost in thoughts. Papa met Lizzie and me at the door and wanted to know how the day went. All I said was, "It went well, and I'm tired."

A week passed and I got a letter from Vernon and he said that Mr. and Mrs. Carrington had invited him down for the week after Christmas, because they are going to have a New Year's Eve party and wanted me to attend. He'd also like to meet the rest of my family. By then, Lizzie had told Papa and Grandpa about him and me, and they said that they were eager to meet Vernon, too. I was so excited. I would have to get a new dress made, and Darla, Grandpa's friend agreed to sew it for me.

As I wrote Vernon back, I couldn't help thinking about what it might mean—the possibility of me leaving Ocoee for good. I knew I would miss Papa and Grandpa dearly, not to mention Lizzie, and all the familiar places and haunts. But it was also crystal clear to me that there was no future here, not for someone like me. So I wrote Vernon that I couldn't wait to see him and was counting the days.

That was the start to our whirlwind courtship. It was love at first sight for both of us and we kept the letters going back and forth between us. I knew I wanted to be with him, no matter what state we lived in.

Vernon didn't waste any time, either. The day after Christmas, he surprised me by coming by the dairy to meet Grandpa and Papa. He said he wanted to see our operation, which pleased them both. Grandpa, who called him "Vern," took him around to show him the herd. They were gone a good, long time. Then Papa and Vern went into the barn to look at all the equipment. They came back chatting amiably.

But that wasn't the end of it. Vernon had expressed an interest in me and they put him through the wringer. Being from Virginia, he was an outsider, and therefore naturally suspect. The fact that the Carrington's vouched for him helped some, but wasn't enough to satisfy Papa and Grandpa. It wasn't until they all went on a turkey shoot together and Vern acquitted himself as a crack shot that they welcomed him as one of them. He had passed muster in their eyes and they were comfortable with him.

I wore my beautiful new dress, a blue velvet gown to the New Year's Eve party at the Carrington's. When the clock chimed midnight, we went out on the side porch and kissed.

Then Vernon got down on one knee and said, "Georgia I love you. Will you marry me? I've already asked your Papa and Grandpa. I can support you and take care of you."

My heart skipped a beat and I felt a flush of joy come over me. "Yes," I said, "Yes, I will marry you."

Before he slipped the engagement ring on my finger, he said, "You know that means you'll be leaving here to join me in Virginia. Are you okay with that?"

I didn't hesitate, "Yes, but I want the wedding to be here."

He nodded. Then he kissed me again, took my hand and said, "Let's tell your Papa and Grandpa.

Vern borrowed Eugene's car and drove to the homestead. When we got there, Papa opened the door. He and Grandpa had been waiting for us and were looking at us expectantly. I threw myself in Papa's arms.

Vernon said, "We have come so we can get your blessings."

Papa held me at arm's length and looked at me searchingly until he saw how happy I was. Then he hugged me again and said, "You have my blessing."

Grandpa stood there with a big smile on his face, but his eyes were moist when he said, "And mine. I am so glad I've been able to be here for this moment."

Vernon said, formally, "Thank you both. We need to set a date."

I looked at him and asked, "Would February 14 be too soon—Valentine's Day?"

"Tomorrow would not be too soon. I already have a job and a house. All I need is my Georgia."

The news of my upcoming marriage quickly became a favorite topic of conversation around town and had a lot of people wagging their tongues disapprovingly. It meant that I would be going away from Ocoee, and that just wasn't what a Southern girl did. You stayed close to your home. It may have been all right for Charlotte Anne Carrington—her family was from up north—but a true born Southerner stayed put.

When customers at the dairy came right out and asked Papa how he felt about it, he always put up a good front, defending me by saying that he was fine with it because Vernon was a good man. But I could tell by how forlorn he looked afterward that it upset him, too.

When it came time for the wedding, Vern arrived two days early, staying at the Carrington's. He came over to our house and brought me a bouquet of pink roses. I was touched that he had remembered my favorite color. We spent the day together, walking down to Starke Lake and looking at the placid water and the birds that were hiding in the lake grasses along the shore.

Vern asked, "It's very pretty here. Are you sure you can leave all this behind?"

I realized, looking across the lake, that something still seemed off. The landscape hadn't recovered from all the havoc and destruction during the massacre.

I turned to him and said, "There is no doubt in my heart."

The day of the wedding arrived, and I was ready to become Mrs. Georgia Brightwell Kambel Stephens. Janie and Eugene came over early, to be my matron of honor and Vern's best man. Darla was there, right on time, to help me get into the dress and veil she had made for me. I had a thought about Essie and wished she could be here, but I knew that was impossible. Darla had brought a bouquet of orange blossoms and greenery for me to carry. I was touched that she was so sweet to me.

We had agreed on a small ceremony at our house, just the family and a few friends—Sarah, David and, yes, even Ned, with a reception in the backyard afterward. Vern, Janie, Eugene and Pastor John stood in front of the fireplace. Darla played the Wedding March on the piano. Papa escorted me out into the living room to Vern who was anxiously waiting. Papa took my hand and put it in Vern's hand and then he sat down on the sofa next to Grandpa and Lizzie. I looked at Vern and he had tears in his eyes. As we said our vows I knew in my heart that this man was the only man for me. Pastor John pronounced us husband and wife and everyone clapped and started to hug and congratulate us.

There were some wedding gifts on the table in the living room and we started to open them. The Carrington's gave us a lovely antique table cloth that had been in their family for a long time. The other gifts were household items that we would need. I whispered to Vern that we would have to pack them tonight for the trip. I was so surprised when Darla brought out a wedding cake that she had made and put it on the dining room table. It was beautiful, and tasted delicious. All the guests had cake and punch.

As they started to leave and say their good-byes, Papa whispered to me, "You two will have supper here with the family."

When everyone else was gone, we had our last family meal together, which included Darla. Janie had actually helped Lizzie prepare food for the supper and we all had a good time.

Then it was time for Vern and me to take off—we were spending our first time together in the Oakland Hotel honeymoon suite. They all hugged us and wished us God speed. It was hard to say good-bye to Papa and Grandpa. I told them how much I loved them, but it didn't make things any easier. We had tears in our eyes because we did not know if we would see each other again.

Vern carried my suit cases to the car.

"Make sure you write to us," Papa called after us from the front porch.

The thought went through my mind that I needed a new journal for Georgia Brightwell Kambel Stephens.

Sunday morning came and it was time for me to take my first train ride. I was excited and I looked around for the last time, as I left my life in Florida for my new life as the wife of Vernon Stephens in Virginia. I thought of my family and friends especially Papa, Grandpa, Essie, Big Jim and Little Jim, and I prayed that the Lord would be with us all until we met again. As the train pulled away from the Oakland Station tears were in my eyes, but with Vern at my side there was also joy in my heart.

EPILOGUE

Altogether, G'ma returned to Ocoee three times—once when Grandpa died just a year and a half after her wedding, another when Lizzie got married three years later, and the last time in 1934 for Papa's funeral. If she wrote down her thoughts and feelings about those occasions, it must have been in another journal that was lost or destroyed. I didn't find any evidence of it in my search through her papers.

I'm not sure why she never set foot in the town again. From comments one of my Ocoee relatives made, an aunt who was willing to talk to me, I got the impression that G'ma and her sisters Lizzie and Janie got mad at each other at her Papa's funeral and said things that couldn't be unsaid. It often happens at funerals, when emotions are high, that family members do or say something that tears the scabs off old wounds, causing new rifts that, in some cases, never heal.

Another possibility is that G'ma was appalled by how little had changed in the town during the decade she was gone. When the subject came up at all, people still acted like they'd done the right thing on that Election Day and during the night of the massacre.

In fact, racist attitudes prevailed in Ocoee for at least another half century. For the next six decades, no African Americans lived in the city, and those who worked there had to be gone by sunset. As late as 1959 a sign at one of the entrances into town told visitors that "Negroes and Dogs Unwelcome."

The KKK remained active, too. During the school integration struggles of the 1960s, it held protest rallies within blocks of the Spring Lake Elementary school. A decade later, there were no blacks living in the city and African Americans were still leery of working there. Not until 1981 did the first African Americans move back to Ocoee.

In 1986, the city hired its first black municipal employee. But when Orlando celebrated its first Martin Luther King holiday in 1986, Ocoee did not. It wasn't until 1998 that it decided to join the rest of the country and honor the man who had done so much for advancing the rights of African Americans.

In the late 1990s and early 2000s, some local residents attempted to affect a kind of reconciliation. The West Orange Reconciliation Task Force dedicated itself to bring to light the history of the riot and promote racial good will in Ocoee. Two local ministers, one black, the other white, co-chaired the task force, and a number of prominent residents, including the daughter of Colonel Salisbury, were members. They held forums and, with the permission of July Perry's family, erected a commemorative gravestone on his pauper's grave in Orlando's Greenwood Cemetery.

But their efforts received mixed receptions at best. While a few of Ocoee's residents welcomed the opportunity to recall the troubled past and tragic events of the 1920 Election Day, the majority wanted nothing to do with revisiting Ocoee's racist history. As an article in the *Wall Street Journal* pointed out at the time, "The city's official slogan is 'Center of Good Living.' Unofficially, though, it has been, 'Let Sleeping Dogs Lie.'

At the time, Ocoee was one of the fastest growing communities in the South. The ranks of its inhabitants had swelled to 22,000, of who about 500 were African Americans, matching the number of those who had been driven out eighty years earlier.

When I finished my thesis, one question remained. Why did Mr. Edwards, "Little Jim," attend G'ma's funeral after all those years? I hadn't felt comfortable contacting him to talk about the massacre, but I was curious about what had brought him back to Ocoee. I called his great granddaughter, Georgia Mae, and told her that I'd like to come for a visit. After checking with him, she said that it would be all right, and that he was looking forward to seeing me.

In the course of doing my research, I had visited the Orlando and Ocoee areas several times, and I took this opportunity to go back there again.

I drove around Ocoee, which looked once again like a sleepy little town with no sign of trouble, and visited Oakland, where the gates to the Mather-Smith's country club could still be seen, although the property was all farm and grazing land now.

In Orlando, I went to the Greenwood Cemetery, where the remains of July Perry and Colonel Sam Salisbury lay within a stone's throw from one another. It was a fitting irony. Salisbury had died in 1974 by a self-inflicted gunshot wound. I don't think his relatives knew of the nearby pauper grave when they buried him. Looking at the commemorative marker on July Perry's grave, I thought about how the remains of those two men, bitter enemies on that horrific day, were reconciled in death occupying the same place in a way that they never were in life.

It was late in 2008, and the first African-American president had just been elected. Many people hoped that things would change for the better and that it would mark the end of our country's shameful racial history.

I paid my respects to both men and drove to Jacksonville to meet with "Little Jim." He was living in a suburb on the southern side of the city, in an integrated neighborhood. I saw white and black kids playing together at a basketball hoop in someone's driveway.

When I got to his house, a white stucco, Florida Ranch-style home, I parked on the street. The property was well taken care of with a palm tree in the front yard and a large live oak tree in back, whose branches reached over the shingle roof. There were flower-beds along the walk and the lawn had just been mowed.

Georgia Mae met me at the door and invited me inside. The en-trance foyer was dark and the house smelled musty. When she ush-ered me into the living room, Mr. Edwards was sitting in a recliner chair, with pillows surrounding him. He looked frailer than the time I had seen him four years earlier, but his eyes sparkled with life and curiosity.

He smiled kindly at me and said, "Excuse me for not getting up, but these old bones ain't as spry as they used to be."

I waved him off. "Thank you for seeing me, Mr. Edwards."

"Call me Jim," he said, gesturing to a nearby chair. "Everyone else does."

I was about to sit when I noticed a series of photographs on the mantle of the fire place. One of them showed an older black man and woman on either side of a young black man in a pastor's gown. They were well dressed and both had gray hair.

From behind me, I heard Jim's voice, "That's my mama, Essie, and my daddy, Big Jim, just after I graduated from the seminary. What happened to us in Ocoee aged them prematurely."

"I didn't realize you were a minister," I offered.

"For nearly sixty years," he said proudly. "I retired at ninety."

I was amazed and would have turned around, but another photo captured my attention. It was of Essie in a more casual dress. Next to her stood a younger white woman, ten years my senior. With a shock, I realized I was looking at G'ma. They both had serious expres-sions on their faces.

"And, yes, that is Mrs. Stephens, my good friend Georgia," came the voice from behind me.

Turning around, I asked, "When was this taken?"

Just then Jim's granddaughter came in with a tray of glasses and a pitcher of iced tea. She gestured to the chair, "Please sit, sit." Then she adjusted Jim's recliner, so he could sit up straight, and serve us both.

Jim took a long sip. Then he leaned back, sighed, and said, "It was taken at the funeral of my daddy." He shook his head, as if to banish the sad memory, and continued, "Your great grandmother first visited us in 1934 after she went to her Papa's funeral in Ocoee. She'd been trying to find us for some time and finally located me because I was listed as an assistant pastor at our church. She was very upset, and not just because she'd lost her Papa, but because of all the memories it brought back, both good and bad. She had argued with her sisters about benefiting from what happened. Lizzie accused her of running away and leaving her in the lurch to care for their ailing Papa alone, and Janie took her side. They didn't part on good terms."

"Didn't her husband come with her?" I asked.

"We met Vernon on subsequent visits," Jim said. "That first time, we spent the whole weekend catching up. It was like we'd never been apart. From then on we communicated by letter and phone, and visited each other. She came to the christening of my children and both of my parents' funerals. It was so good to have her here when my mama passed. She was a great comfort to me."

Tears welled up in his eyes at the memory and he remained quiet for a while. Then he said, "After that we wrote each other once a week, come rain or shine."

He gestured to Georgia Mae, who went to a desk in a corner and brought back a big box. She put it on the coffee table and opened it.

It was filled with letters in envelopes, neatly organized. Taking one of them, I recognized G'ma's neat handwriting with the little flourishes.

"When I didn't get a letter from her one week, I knew something was wrong," Jim said. "I tried to call her, but there was no answer, so I telephoned your uncle and he told me that she had died. I wasn't sure I could make it up to Virginia, but when I heard the funeral would be in Ocoee, I knew I had to be there." He sighed. "I'd never gone back, but I wanted to pay my last respects."

I said, "I'm so glad you did."

Jim smiled a little. "I didn't think I'd outlive her, but we will see each other soon." His face radiated acceptance and serenity.

We continued our conversation a little longer but didn't talk about when he and his parents left Ocoee. I didn't want to raise any more painful memories, and I could tell he was tiring. Georgia Mae caught my eye and I nodded to her.

But before I left, I had to ask him one more thing. "In her journal G'ma mentioned a song she heard you and your mama sing that made a big impression on her. Do you remember what that was?"

He closed his eyes and for a moment his face took on a child-like expression. When he opened them again, they danced with pleasure. He knew exactly what I was talking about. He looked at me slyly, with an almost mischievous expression, and started to sing, at first softly, then with rising joy:

> *You sift-a the meal, you give me the husk.*
> *You cook-a the bread, you give me the crust.*
> *Then you Juba up, Juba down,*
> *Juba all around town.*

Why We Wrote the Book

Beginning in the 1940s, we grew up in the small all white town of Ocoee located in Central Florida. Since our lives were centered in this West Orange County community, we accepted our daily lives as being normal and typical. In many ways, we grew up as innocent and ignorant as Georgia, our protagonist. We did realize that there were no blacks in our town. Those who worked there during the day, were gone by sundown. No black person would be caught in Ocoee after dark. While Southerners are proud of their history and keep much of it alive orally, we never heard any facts, only idealized gossip, about the riot, that occurred on Election Day, 1920. Teachers sharing local history in our schools never mentioned it.

As time passed and we grew into adulthood our interest in uncovering the truth of the historical past of Ocoee became more important to us. It turned almost into an obsession. We utilized all the local sources that were available to us to begin putting the pieces together that surrounded the Ocoee Riot. Much to our surprise, we discovered that Ocoee was not the only town in Florida that experienced much unrest and upheaval in the black communities.

Starting in 2008, after years of silence, some public discussions started to take place about the Ocoee 1920 Election Day riot through the efforts of a reconciliation task force in the community. Talks and symposiums were held in several locations in Ocoee. In one meeting at a local book store, tempers began to flare when "massacre" was used to describe the riot. Some members of the task force whose family members had been directly involved in the events that happened said that the word "massacre" was too strong. Despite 80 years having passed, it was still a sore subject for many.

The advent of the computer age assisted us in expanding our historical research. New information concerning the issues that surrounded the volatile 1920 Presidential Election throughout Florida and the United States became readily accessible. The culmination of this information was important in our understanding of what led to the tragic events of the Ocoee Massacre and its aftermath.

After years of research, we decided to write this book to shed some light on what happened. We decided to create a fictionalized story, told from the perspective of a young, white girl who bore witness to what occurred. The account from the point of view of the black participants and victims remains to be written.

We have strived to be as accurate as we can in describing the lives of the actual people who lived in and around the Ocoee area during the period from 1913 through 1927. Any factual errors we may have committed are the result of having to choose among conflicting accounts of what happened and our own oversights. We hope that they will not diminish the intent or meaning of our narrative.

We believe the time has come to draw back the veil for good that has shrouded the Ocoee Riot in obscurity and hidden the reality of what happened from too many people for too long.

We continue to believe in Voltaire's dictum that "To the living we owe respect, but to the dead we owe only the truth."

Myra Kinnie & Gail Waxman
Ocoee, Florida
January 2017

ACKNOWLEDGMENTS

As we did research for the story, many dedicated historians made it possible for us to gather this research by scouring archives of old real estate records, vital statistics records, various newspaper articles, books and college research papers. The following are some of the more helpful organizations, books, research papers and visual aids:

Organizations

The Winter Garden History Center, Winter Garden, Florida.

The Withers Maguire History Center, Ocoee, Florida.

The Orange County History Center, Orlando, Florida.

The Florida Historical Society, Cocoa, Brevard County, Florida.

Mather's Library at the University of Florida and Dr. James Cusack, Gainesville, Florida;

Albertson's Library, Old Newspaper Section, Orlando, Florida.

Harry T. & Harriette V. Moore Memorial Park, Mims, Florida.

Museum of the Apopkans, Apopka, Florida.

Orange County, Florida Property Appraiser's Office and Website.

Orange County, Florida Comptroller's Office and Website.

Stetson Kennedy's Archives of events of life in the KKK as a young man, St. Augustine, Florida. (Sandra K. Parks, a St. Augustine Historian, most graciously opened the Archives to us).

Books

Bacon, Eve, *Oakland the Early Years*, The Mickler House Publishers, Chuluota, Florida, 1974.

Bacon, Eve, *A Centennial History, Vol. I*, The Mickler House Publishers, Chuluota, Florida, 1973.

Bacon, Eve, *A Centennial History, Vol. II*, The Mickler House Publishers, Chuluota, Florida, 1977.

Blackman, William, PhD, LLD, *History of Orange County Florida*, The Mickler House Publishers, 1973.

Jones & Hawes, *Step It Down*, The University of Georgia Press, 1972.

Gonzales, Sharon, *Justice Wrapped in Mercy*, JS New Publications, Inc., Apopka, Florida, 2007.

Maguire, Nancy Lillian, *The History of Ocoee and its Pioneers*, Ocoee Historical Commission, Ocoee, Florida, 2009.

Newton, Michael, *The Invisible Empire*, University Press of Florida, 2001.

Ortiz, Paul, *Emancipation Betrayed: The Hidden History of Black Organizing and White Violence in Florida from Reconstruction to the Bloody Election of 1920*, University of California Press, 2005.

Shofner, Jerrell H., *History of Apopka*, Apopka Historical Society, 1982.

Ste. Claire, Dana, *Cracker*, University Press of Florida, 2006;

Tebeau & Marina, A *History of Florida, Third Edition*, University of Miami Press, 1999.

Whitner, J.N., *Early Settlers of Orange County, Florida*, C.E. Howard Publisher, Orlando, Florida, 1915.

Papers and Articles

Cardwell, Kathy Amick Fugue, *Racial Justice: Orange County 1920-1970*, Master of Liberal Studies, 1992.

Dabbs, Lester J., *The Ocoee Race Riot*, Master of Arts Thesis, Stetson University, 1969.

Fleming, James R., *Orange County Race Riot*, 2002.

Parrish, Dorothy, *The Ocoee Race Riot; A Historical Study*, Florida Technological University, 1970's.

Parry, Kathryn K., *Constructing African American Histories in Central Florida*, Master of Arts Thesis, University of Central Florida, 2008.

FL A&M University, FL State & the University of FL, *The Rosewood Report History*, submitted to the Florida Board of Regents December 22, 1993.

The Weekly Challenger in Hidden History, *The Ocoee Massacre*, 2015.

Visual Aids

Griffith, D.W., *The Birth of a Nation*, 1919.

Sandra Krasa & Bianca White, *Ocoee Legacy of the Election Day Massacre*, Wise Eye Media, Inc., 2008.

We want to give very special thanks to our husbands, Richard and Roy, who put up with our mutual obsession for such a long time.

Finally, we wish to thank Chris Angermann of Bardolf & Company for his unwavering support and expertise in shepherding the book into print, as well as giving us direction in telling the story. We could not have done it without him.